From the Nancy Drew Files

THE CASE: Investigate the mysterious drowning of Rina Charles, a student at San Diego University.

CONTACT: Susan Victors. *Nancy's old friend has grave suspicions about her sorority sister's "accident".*

SUSPECTS: Fran Kelly. *She is driven by ambition and jealousy. She hated Rina's success, and now she hates Nancy.*

Lori Westerly. *The lovely contender for the Olympic team has a knack for attracting violence.*

Alice Clark. *The drab bookworm is an expert in judo techniques—especially deadly pressure points.*

COMPLICATIONS: Nancy's cover has been blown— now the hunted is stalking the hunter.

Nancy Drew Files™ available in Armada

THE NANCY DREW FILES™

Case 19

Sisters in Crime

Carolyn Keene

Armada
An Imprint of HarperCollins*Publishers*

First published in the USA in 1988 by
Simon & Schuster Inc.
First published in Great Britain
in Armada in 1991

Armada is an imprint of
HarperCollins Children's Books,
part of HarperCollins Publishers Ltd,
77–85 Fulham Palace Road,
Hammersmith, London W6 8JB

Printed and bound in Great Britain by
HarperCollins Manufacturing, Glasgow

Sisters in Crime

Chapter

One

"NANCY! YOU'RE HERE!" Susan Victors reached out and hugged her old friend Nancy Drew, after Nancy walked through security at the San Diego airport.

"I don't know what I would have done if you hadn't been able to come!" Susan exclaimed. "Thank you *so* much."

"I'm happy to be here, Susan," Nancy responded as she returned the warm hug and then stood back to look at her old friend.

"Tan, in February!" Nancy exclaimed, pointing to the deep golden coloring on Susan's arms beneath her short-sleeved pink T-shirt. "You

1

look wonderful! Now I know why you wanted to go to college in California!"

Susan, who had always been quiet and studious at River Heights High, looked very different to Nancy now that she was a student at San Diego University.

"And you cut your hair," Nancy added, looking at her friend's short, dark curly hair. All through high school, Susan had worn her hair in a long ponytail. "It looks great."

Glancing down at her own clothes—an oversize gray cable-knit sweater with a bright blue cowl-neck sweater under it, and navy pants, Nancy said, "It's still winter in River Heights."

"And you *still* look wonderful," Susan said, looking at her fair-skinned friend with the shoulder-length reddish blond hair. "No matter what the season." Nancy had a slim build and was perhaps four inches taller than Susan's five feet three.

As they headed toward the baggage claim area, Susan said, "I can't tell you how much I appreciate your coming, Nancy. I really do need you." Turning and looking at Susan's eyes, Nancy saw the pain that she had heard in her friend's voice during her urgent phone call the day before.

When they were seated in Susan's little yellow car, Susan turned to Nancy. "You're the only one who can help me," she said softly. "The only one who can possibly uncover the truth about Rina's death."

Nancy nodded her head. "I'll do my best," she promised.

Susan pointed to the book, *Scuba-diving Safety,* that Nancy was holding on her lap. "I see you've started to do your research already."

"I wanted to make sure I'd understand all the technicalities and jargon," Nancy said. "The police still believe it was an accident?"

Susan nodded. "They say she was washed up with an empty air tank near the place she likes to dive—I mean, where she used to like to dive." Susan shook her head as she corrected herself. Nancy could see it was hard for Susan to believe that her roommate, Rina, was really dead.

"They found her on the beach wearing her wet suit and weight belt," Susan said sadly. "They say that she must have read the air gauge incorrectly. That's all."

"But that's not all?" Nancy prodded.

Nancy Drew, at eighteen, was already established as a top-notch private detective. For years everyone in her hometown had known of her excellent work, especially that done in cooperation with her father, Carson Drew, the famous criminal lawyer.

Now her reputation and skills were taking her farther from home. Southern California was a long way from River Heights, where she had recently solved a mystery at the exclusive River Heights Country Club.

"I have no hard evidence, Nancy. I wish I

did." Susan sighed. "But I *know* her death wasn't that simple," she said with determination. "I just *know* there's more to it than a poorly read air gauge."

"Tell me what you think," Nancy said, encouraging her gently.

Although Susan had the car keys out and in her hand, she made no attempt to start driving. Slowly she began the story that had brought her friend halfway across the country.

"Rina Charles had been my roommate since last fall, when we lived in the dorm together. This semester we were *both* invited to join Delta Phi, so we were happy we could continue rooming together." Susan took a deep breath. "I guess I told you this on the phone yesterday."

"It's okay. Just give me any information that you can."

"Well, Delta Phi is considered to be 'the' sorority to be in, and when we lived in the dorm, Rina could only think about whether she was going to be asked to pledge. Her mother had been a sorority member twenty-five years ago, and I think it was important to Rina not to let her mother down. That was how she saw it, anyway."

Nancy slipped off her oversize sweater and put it in the backseat so she would be more comfortable as she listened to Susan.

"When the sorority bids first went out, Rina didn't get one, and she was crushed. Someone let it slip that she didn't have 'the right image.' But soon, I think it was the very next day, the girls of Delta Phi changed their minds. It seems that if you're a legacy—if your mom or some other relative has been in the sorority—they *have* to give you a bid. It's some sort of rule, so Rina's hurt was for no reason."

Listening to Susan, Nancy couldn't help but think of Bess and George, her two closest girl-friends. They had been friends for years. Nancy knew how heartbroken she would feel if anything happened to either of them and could appreciate the pain that Susan was in.

"How hard for Rina to know that she was being asked to join only because the rules made them ask her." Nancy shook her auburn head sadly.

"Yeah, it was pretty rough," Susan admitted. "And I had even suggested to Rina that we both forget the whole sorority thing and just live in the dorm. Wait until you see the campus, Nancy, it's so beautiful. But," Susan continued, "Rina wouldn't hear of it. She wanted to be a Delta Phi more than anything in the world."

"How was it after you moved into the sorority house?" Nancy inquired, leaning back against the locked car door.

"That's the beginning of the strange part," Susan said curiously. "Some of the members were a little rude to Rina, but most of them were nice. There's this small group of six sorority sisters who, along with the president, Lori Westerly, pretty much run things. You know, they're all officers, and assign rooms, and that type of thing. And they're pretty snobby. I heard it was that group who didn't want Rina in the sorority in the first place. Well, suddenly, right after we moved in, Rina started hanging around with that crowd."

"That is strange," Nancy agreed.

"I mean, one day she's being told she isn't good enough, and the next day she's best friends with all the officers," Susan said. "It was really weird. Anyway, for that short time Rina was very happy!"

"Do you think that being in this inner circle is somehow related to what happened to Rina?" Nancy asked.

"I don't know. And that's what I mean by having so little evidence. But a week ago Wednesday Rina told me that there was something wrong going on in the sorority." Susan looked at Nancy as she added, her voice shaking, "Something *dangerously* wrong."

"Dangerously wrong?" Nancy said, encouraging her friend. She could see that it wasn't easy for Susan to talk about this.

Susan nodded. "Those were her exact words. Rina said that she couldn't tell me, or anyone else about it yet, but she would soon." Susan took a deep breath before she continued. "She said she *had* to tell someone what she knew."

Looking down, Susan added, "She sounded very desperate, Nan."

"Do you think she talked to anyone else?" Nancy asked.

Susan shook her head. "No. And you're the first person I've told," Susan said as she put her key in the ignition. "I just haven't known who to trust."

"And you never did find out what it was that was 'dangerously wrong'?" Nancy inquired.

Shaking her head, Susan stared out the front window at the huge airport parking lot. "That was on Wednesday. By Friday, Rina was dead."

"And you think—" Nancy prodded gently.

As Susan looked back at Nancy, tears were visible in her eyes. "I think Rina knew something that she died never having told anyone." Susan turned the key in the ignition. "I think" —she hesitated—"I think Rina knew something that got her killed."

Chapter

Two

THE SORORITY PHOTOGRAPH Susan showed Nancy pictured forty-two members. Nancy studied it during the drive to the campus, memorizing names and reminding herself how deceptive looks can be.

"See Fran Kelly?" Susan asked.

"Yes—here with the bangs?" Nancy asked, pointing. "Is her hair tied back in a ribbon?"

"Always. She must have a thousand of them."

"Is she a friend? She has a nice smile."

Watching the road, Susan shook her head. "No, not a friend," she said. "She's the person I'm most afraid of."

"Why is that?" Nancy asked, peering out the

window at the Pacific Ocean, inviting white sand beaches, and palm trees that lined the highway.

"On the very day of Rina's funeral, Fran came to my room and asked if she could move in with me. She said she was having trouble with her roommate and wanted to switch to a different room."

"How did you handle it?" Nancy asked.

"I told her that it was a little soon for me to have a new roommate. That I needed some time. The truth is that I don't like Fran much and don't want to live with her."

"How come?"

"A lot of reasons, but mostly because she never even spoke to me before that day. I was surprised she even remembered my name when she came to my room. She's the most stuck-up person in Delta Phi, and only wants to be in Lori's group."

"I can understand how awful you must have felt," Nancy said sympathetically.

"And she didn't even seem sad that Rina had died. I mean she went to the memorial service and everything, but I'm sure it was just because that was where everyone else was going to be that day. Even the girls who didn't like Rina didn't want to see her dead. Everyone else, with the exception of Fran, was very upset."

As they pulled onto the sprawling campus, Nancy could hardly believe that such a beautiful, peaceful-looking place might be hiding something as sinister as murder.

She looked back down at the photograph on her lap. Rina Charles had short, straight hair, one side cut slightly shorter than the other. She was looking straight at the camera as all the other girls were. Nothing in particular distinguished her from the forty-one other girls. Nancy also looked closely at those girls that Susan said made up Lori's inner circle: Pam, Jan, Ellen, Kathy, and Johanna.

She felt anxious to meet all the people in this picture. Could one of these seemingly normal girls be involved in murder? The photograph would never tell her. Nancy would have to rely on the girls themselves to do that. She needed the guilty person to make a mistake, and she had to be there when it happened.

Nancy straightened the skirt of the denim dress she wore, took a deep breath, and stepped into the Delta Phi dining room. It was a large attractive room, with green-and-white-print wallpaper and six wooden tables that each seated eight.

Slipping into the seat that Susan had saved for her, Nancy looked around at the girls as dinner was being served. Susan pointed out Lori Westerly at the center table. Nancy would have recognized her anywhere. Lori was very tall, perhaps five feet ten inches tall, and had a strikingly strong athletic body that reminded Nancy of her friend George, who loved almost all sports. But

Lori, unlike George, was someone who made the most of her beauty. Wearing deep purple linen shorts and a matching sleeveless top, she was made up to perfection to set off her blond beauty.

Five other girls sat with her, all noticeably attractive. Pam, sitting to the right of Lori, was talking enthusiastically, gesturing with a ketchup-tipped french fry in her hand. Nancy caught one sentence of what she said. "I told him, 'You better apologize, right now, kid! You have no idea who you're dealing with.'" The other girls were listening and nodding in agreement as they ate. "You could buy that bookstore if he treats you like that again," Johanna said. "Let him know who you are."

"You're really welcome to stay here, Nancy," Debbie said warmly, interrupting Nancy's thoughts.

Nancy looked at the friendly redheaded girl seated across the table from her.

"I'm from the Midwest, too," Debbie continued. "And when I first saw this campus, I *knew* I wanted to go here. Warm sunshine, beautiful ocean, cute guys—"

"I thought you came here to get a fine higher education," Debbie's roommate, Patty, commented.

"And a fine higher education," Debbie tacked on.

Nancy laughed along with the others. "It does seem fabulous here," Nancy answered. "The little I've seen of it so far. I've got a cute guy back home, though, so *that* part I'm not really interested in."

"Ah, a loyal woman." Patty teased more. "How honorable."

Nancy chatted with the people at her table as she continued her meal. Patty and Debbie shared the room that was right next to Susan's, and Nancy knew that Susan liked them.

The noisy dining-room chatter ended when Lori Westerly knocked on her water glass with a fork and stood up.

"Remember we have a Valentine's Day party here this Friday afternoon with Zeta Psi fraternity, right after classes. We'll need a decorating crew. Can I see hands of volunteers?"

Nancy looked around the room as half a dozen hands waved, and Jan, at Lori's table, made a note of their names.

"How about we all dress in red and white?" a voice called out from behind Nancy.

Nancy noticed Lori glance at her table where, very subtly, two of the inner circle, Pam and Ellen, shook their heads no.

"Optional dress code," Lori declared. "Any other announcements?"

Next to Nancy, Susan rose. "I'd like to introduce my cousin, Nancy Drew, who's visiting campus this week to see if she's interested in coming to SDU."

Nancy rose to greet everyone, and as she did

so, she scanned the room. While most of the sorority sisters nodded hello and smiled, there were a few people who didn't even look at her. And some, Nancy sensed, just looked at her to size her up, just as she was doing, trying to gather information about them.

"Don't we have a guest rule in effect here?" someone called out.

As Nancy sat down, she looked at the girl who had asked that question. Her black hair was tied back at the nape of her neck with a gray ribbon. Her eyes, the same color gray, steel gray, as the ribbon, had observed Nancy carefully when she was introduced. Smiling, she looked at Nancy. "Nothing personal," she said warmly.

"Which guest rule is that?" Lori asked as Susan wrote the letters F.K. on the table next to Nancy's plate with her finger. Yes, Nancy knew from the photo that she was Fran Kelly, and casually looked away from Susan, hoping nobody else had seen her too obvious message.

"The three-day rule. We talked about it at the last meeting."

"That rule wasn't for out-of-towners," Patty said loudly so she could be heard by everyone in the room. "It was meant for people who live on campus, or in San Diego. We didn't want friends crashing here whenever they wanted."

Nancy saw the girls at the head table give questioning glances around the table. Ellen leaned over and whispered something to Lori.

13

"I think we need to be consistent with our rules," someone behind Nancy called out. Nancy looked over her shoulder to see a girl whose last name she could remember as Miller speaking. She would have to study that photograph more, so she could identify everyone.

When more people began to call out their opinions, Lori tapped her glass again and said, "Susan, we'll let you know how long your cousin can stay. Sorry, Nancy. In the meantime, you're very welcome."

"Thank you," Nancy said politely. As she looked at the cups of chocolate ice cream that were being passed around the table for dessert, Nancy thought, Yes, indeed, I am certainly being checked out.

Nancy had counted forty-one girls at dinner —forty-two including herself, which meant that nobody was absent. If Susan's theory is right, Nancy considered, that Rina's death was not an accident, but a murder, then there must have been a *reason* for it. And if the reason is related to whatever it was that Rina found out when she was admitted to the inner circle, then there are people in this room who know what that reason is. And it's my job to find it out.

Nancy got a chill as she took the last bite of her ice cream and thought, It's my job to figure out if there is a murderer sitting in this room!

Chapter

Three

Susan's room on the second floor of the large sorority house was one of the smaller ones, and the two beds, two dressers, and two desks nearly filled it.

"So someone wants to get rid of me in three days," Nancy mused as she locked the door after she and Susan entered the room.

"Don't take it personally," Susan said. "Nobody could possibly know why you're here. Your idea to be my cousin is a perfect cover."

Looking at the colorful photos of marine life that hung around the room, Nancy mumbled, "We'll see."

"Rina took all those photos with her underwater camera," Susan said. "Aren't they beautiful?"

"Very." Nancy nodded, studying a school of shimmering orange-green fish.

Turning away from the photographs, Nancy sat on a desk chair and said, "Tell me more about Rina. *Anything* might be helpful."

Sitting across from Nancy on her desk chair, Susan began, "Well, she was an oceanography student, and she was mainly taking classes related to that, like marine biology. She also loved to swim and deep-sea dive. She grew up out here in Southern California, and she dove probably two, three times a week."

"Was she doing well in her classes?" Nancy asked.

"Fine, as far as I know," Susan said.

"Did Rina have a boyfriend?" Nancy asked.

"No." Susan shook her head. "Not here. I think she had somebody she liked last year in high school, but he's at Berkeley this year. She talked to him on the phone every once in a while. I don't think it was a really big deal. Not like you and Ned," Susan said, referring to Nancy's boyfriend of many years. "How are you two doing, by the way?"

Nancy smiled as she thought of Ned Nickerson. "You know, it's kind of amazing that after all these years, I still think he's the greatest." Folding her legs under her, Nancy added, "Sometimes it's hard with him away at school

—he goes to Emerson College—and me traveling around so much, but we manage to stay in touch." Quietly Nancy added, "And in love. We're doing just fine."

Susan smiled back. "When you talk to him, tell him I said hi. I do miss the old gang."

Nancy nodded and absentmindedly picked up a pencil that lay on the desk in front of her.

"There was this one guy that Rina was friendly with," Susan said. "But they weren't dating or anything. He's a part-time student. He works for the San Diego Institute of Oceanography and takes care of all their underwater equipment. From the way she talked about him, I think they were good friends."

"What's his name?" Nancy asked.

"Ira." Susan closed her eyes, obviously searching her memory. "Ira—Ira something. I can't remember his last name. Sorry."

"Did you ever meet him?"

"No. He never visited her here." Susan thought for a minute before she added, "I have a feeling that Rina might have been afraid that he wouldn't have 'the right image' either, so she never brought him around. Maybe that's why. I don't know."

Nancy tapped the eraser end of the pencil against her teeth. "And the place he works, the Oceanography Institute, do you know where it is?"

"Yeah. Not far from here. We could drive out

there tomorrow. I don't have any classes until eleven o'clock on Mondays."

"Good," Nancy said.

"So, with her classes and diving and being treasurer of the sorority, she was pretty busy," Susan said, continuing her description of Rina's life.

"Treasurer?" Nancy looked startled.

"Didn't I mention that?" Susan asked.

"No. You said she was in with Lori and the other officers, but you didn't mention that Rina was elected treasurer."

"Gosh, I'm sorry, Nance. Actually, she wasn't elected. Lori appointed her after the last treasurer got mono and had to go home. It was supposed to be just until we could hold an election. As a pledge, she really couldn't be an officer."

"So that must mean that Rina had access to sorority bank accounts and financial records?" Nancy inquired.

"I suppose so," Susan said apologetically. "It never occurred to me that that could be important. Do you think it is?" Susan asked.

"Could be," Nancy stated simply. "Could be. But we're just beginning, so I have no way of knowing yet what's really important."

"Rina kept her paperwork in a green file box that was right there," Susan said, pointing to an empty spot on Rina's desk. "But even before her body had been found, Lori came and got it."

"Hmm," Nancy said. "I hope I've got more than three days to figure this one out."

Every type of underwater animal greeted Nancy and Susan as they entered the experimental aquarium early the following morning.

The girls went straight to the diving facility, hoping to find someone named Ira. At the overhaul and repair area was a young man fixing some rubber tubing that was attached to a breathing regulator.

"Excuse me," Nancy said.

Without looking up, the young man answered, "Be with you in a minute."

As Susan watched him work, Nancy examined the well-organized area. On one wall hung many different styles and sizes of fins, snorkels, and diving masks. Lined up on the floor were the air tanks. Taking a pressure gauge that was attached to a tank she had picked up, Nancy looked at it carefully. Could Rina think there was more air left, but really be out? she wondered. She turned the gauge over and examined it, looking for any way to tamper with it.

"Yes. Can I help you?" the man turned to Susan and asked.

"We're looking for someone named Ira," Susan said.

"I'm someone named Ira," he answered. "And you are someone named—"

19

"Susan Victors," Susan said. Nancy could tell that Susan immediately liked Ira. Despite her shyness, Susan was smiling at him warmly. Ira was small and muscular, with sandy-colored hair and sparkling dark brown eyes. He looked about twenty years old. Nancy could see an instant attraction between him and Susan.

"This is Nancy Drew," Susan said, introducing her. "My, uh, cousin. We wanted to talk to you if you have some time."

Ira nodded hello to Nancy and said, "I've got a class coming in soon, but until they show up, I'd be happy to talk."

Susan took a breath, then said quietly, "Rina Charles was my roommate and friend."

"Oh, *that* Susan," Ira said. "I'm glad to meet you, Susan. Rina was my friend, too. I guess you know that," he added.

"Yes." Susan nodded.

"I've thought of her every day since her death," Ira said sadly. "Rina was a fine diver and a *safe* diver," he added, shaking his head. "Not like some other people around here. That's why her accident was so outrageous." Pointing out the opened window, Ira said sadly, "It happened just south of the pier, beyond the seawater pumps. I look at that spot all the time."

Nancy listened quietly and then asked Ira, "Could it have been an error in the air pressure gauge? That's what Susan told me the police say."

"I guess it's possible," Ira said to Nancy. "But Rina always checked her equipment out carefully. She even had me look things over. She was *very* thorough."

"How did her equipment look to you that day?" Nancy asked.

"She didn't come by here that day, so I can't say for certain what equipment she used. She was a responsible diver, though, I *can* say that for certain!

"Oh, no," Ira exclaimed as he looked out the window. "Here comes my next class. Why do beginners always look like they've never seen the ocean before?"

They all laughed as they watched a small group of students approach the diving facility. "You know the thing that gets me, though, the part I really don't understand?" Ira said, thinking of Rina again.

"What?" both girls asked at the same time.

"Where was her partner?" Ira asked angrily as he reached over to the pile of fins and began sorting them for the incoming divers. "When Rina didn't come up, why didn't her buddy report it? That's the part I can't understand."

"Maybe she dove alone," Susan suggested.

"Never!" Ira insisted. "That's rule number one of scuba diving, and Rina was too smart and careful to ever go out there alone." He was gripping a fin with both hands as he said, "There was someone with her that day, I can *promise*

21

you that. At least, when she began the dive, anyway."

"You mean—" Nancy began to ask Ira.

"I mean Rina Charles would never dive alone!" Ira said emphatically.

Nancy could see the shocked look on Susan's pale face. They both were amazed by this piece of information.

Ira turned to Nancy and Susan as the other people entered the small area. "I need to get to work. I'm really glad I met you both." Looking at Susan, Ira added, "I hope I'll see you again soon."

Silently Susan looked up at Ira, then she and Nancy headed out the door. Nancy saw that all her friend had managed was a nod and a slight smile.

Outside, Susan put her hands up to her face. "Someone knew Rina was underwater and never reported it!" she said.

Nancy placed her hand gently on her friend's back. "That's the person we have to find," she said with determination.

Susan shoved her hands into the pockets of her khaki shorts as she looked at Nancy. She was greatly upset. "Someone knew Rina was there underwater, and never even checked to see if she was alive or dead."

"Maybe they did," Nancy said sadly. "Maybe they checked to make sure she was *dead.*"

Chapter

Four

How will I find out who the other swimmer was? Nancy asked herself as she strolled around the SDU campus while Susan was in class.

As Nancy returned to the sorority house, Jan Miller, whom Nancy remembered Susan describing as Lori Westerly's best friend, was sitting on the front steps reading a book. "What do you think so far?" Jan asked as Nancy approached.

"The campus? It's beautiful," Nancy replied truthfully. She took a seat on the bottom step near Jan. "I went over to the ocean this morning."

"The Pacific is terrific, eh?"

23

Nancy nodded. "Do you do any diving?" she asked Jan.

"Deep-sea diving, or from a board?"

"Deep-sea. Scuba diving."

"Not me. And if I ever had, I don't know if I'd be interested in it now after what happened to poor Rina Charles."

Nancy didn't want to sound anxious to talk about Rina's death. Casually, she agreed, "Yeah, that was really terrible. Was Rina a good friend of yours, too?"

"Of mine?" Jan sounded surprised. Nancy knew that Jan was a member of what Susan called the "inner circle," the group that Rina had gotten friendly with for a short time. "I liked her okay, I guess. But I wouldn't exactly call her a friend. I got to know her pretty well because she followed Lori around." Jan closed the book that was on her lap, and she looked as if she were about to leave.

"They say it was an accident," Nancy said, leaning back on the stairs and trying to sound only slightly interested. "Maybe a faulty air tank, or maybe Rina's error."

"Probably Lori didn't tell Rina to put air in the tank," Jan said, stretching. "So she didn't."

"Was Rina very dependent on Lori?" Nancy asked innocently, ignoring Jan's nasty sarcasm.

"Very!" Jan said, standing. "Rina worshiped Lori."

Nancy, too, stood up and walked up the front steps to stand next to Jan.

"Rina was nice and all," Jan added, clutching her book close to her body. "I don't mean to say anything unkind about her, but she just didn't know her own mind." As the two of them headed into the sorority house, Jan said, "And that can get you in trouble in this world."

Several people were filing into the dining room, and Jan explained, "Lunch is always buffet. You can just go in and help yourself." Then she started up the stairs.

"Thanks." Nancy said, and suddenly realized that she was very hungry from her morning walk around campus.

In the dining room, a dozen or so of the sorority sisters were eating, some were chatting, some were sitting alone and reading. Nancy helped herself to cold cuts and salad, glanced around, and wondered a little self-consciously where to sit. But before she finished filling her plate, Patty came by and invited Nancy to join her.

Patty, dark-haired with glasses, believed that Nancy really was visiting the campus. She was generous in giving Nancy advice about good instructors. In a few moments Pam and Ellen, two of Lori's inner circle, sat down with them. Interesting, Nancy thought, this clique wants to check on me as much as I want to check on them.

Lori herself passed by the table and said hello to her friends. Then, addressing Nancy, she said, "I don't know if you're busy this afternoon, but I'm going for a swim at about two o'clock, if you'd like to join me."

"I'd love it. Thanks," Nancy said, delighted to have the opportunity to spend time with Lori.

"Meet you on the porch then," Lori said, and waved goodbye.

Lunch finished quickly as people raced to go to their afternoon classes. Nancy was walking out of the dining room alone when Fran Kelly approached her. "You're so obvious," Fran said with a scowl.

"Pardon me?" Nancy asked.

"Obvious," Fran repeated, standing in front of Nancy. "I *know* what you're up to."

Looking directly into Fran Kelly's cold gray eyes, Nancy asked, "And what am I up to?"

"Coy, aren't we?" Fran said back like a shot. "Okay, I'll tell you, Nancy Drew. You're trying to impress *just* the right people, so you can get into this sorority."

"I'm not even in the school yet, Fran," Nancy said calmly.

Fran squinted her eyes and gritted her teeth as she said in a whisper, "Well, you can just watch it, because I'm on to you. I know your type, Nancy Drew."

As Nancy watched Fran walk away, she understood Susan's mistrust of the girl. Fran sure doesn't want me around, Nancy thought as she headed upstairs, wondering if Fran had felt the same about Rina Charles.

Nancy remembered her dad quoting another famous attorney. "There's a big difference between being glad someone is dead and killing them." Nancy reminded herself of this as she entered Susan's room to change into her swimsuit.

"Thanks for inviting me," Nancy said as she got into Lori's car at two o'clock.

"I'm happy to have the company," Lori said. "I do this swim nearly every day—two miles. And I almost never get anyone to join me. If it's too much for you, just do what you can."

Nancy glanced at Lori's beautiful face. She was wearing only a dark blue racer's bathing suit and shorts, and Nancy could see how muscular her legs, arms, and back were. Lori was in excellent physical shape. She was, Nancy knew, one of the finest high board divers on the SDU swim team.

"I don't get the regular workout you do," Nancy said modestly. "But I'm pretty sure I can keep up for the swim."

"You look like you can keep up with just about anything," Lori exclaimed.

Glancing at Lori as she pulled into the parking lot, Nancy said, "Thank you—I guess."

"Oh, it's a compliment!" Lori insisted, getting out of her car and grabbing a bright green beach bag from the backseat. "You're in great shape. I had a feeling you'd join me for a swim."

Nancy picked up her backpack and hopped out, too. Lori seemed warm to her and quite different from what she would have expected from Susan's description of her.

"I think I'm good at reading people," Lori said. "During rush week, I can say hello to someone and know if she's right for Delta Phi. Something either clicks or it doesn't."

The two girls began to walk down the clean sandy beach toward a spot just south of the pier beyond the seawater pumps—the place where Rina Charles's body had been found.

As Nancy was thinking about how to bring the conversation around to Rina, Lori did it herself.

"This is where they found my friend," she said sadly.

"I was sorry to hear about her death," Nancy said sympathetically. "Susan told me about Rina."

"Yeah. It was rough," Lori murmured. "I miss her. She really supported my dreams."

"How?" Nancy asked.

Tossing her bag over her shoulder, Lori explained, "There's this one diving coach who everyone knows is the best in the country. His name is Lee Logan Marlow. He's been training Olympic divers for ten years now. If you get accepted into his summer training camp, you're just about assured a place on the U.S. team. Rina was the one person who really understood how important it was for me to work with him." Lori stopped and looked out at the dark, still ocean as she said, "It's more important than anything else in my life."

"How do you qualify to train with him?" Nancy asked.

"I try out in April. I tried out two summers ago and didn't get in."

"That must have been hard," Nancy said, feeling sympathy for Lori.

"They said that my form was good," Lori explained. "But I didn't have the strength. Now I do. I've been lifting weights and swimming regularly, and I've really built up my power. I get pretty good training on the SDU team, too." Walking down on the hard, wet sand now, the waves touched the girls' feet. It felt cool and wonderful, and Nancy was looking forward to getting into the water.

"I was naive last time," Lori said.

"What do you mean?" Nancy asked.

"I didn't realize that it's *who* you know that gets you in places. And," Lori said with a grin, "money helps—a lot. Plenty of divers have good skills. Plenty."

Lori pointed to a rocky area on the sand, and she said, "We can put our stuff down over there."

"I wish you luck with all this, Lori," Nancy said, dropping her backpack in the sand behind the rocks. She felt a great respect for Lori and enjoyed talking to her. Lori was right. Sometimes things just clicked between people.

After pulling her green hooded sweatshirt over her head, Nancy felt a hand circle her wrist, a strong hand, gripping her hard. She followed the hairy arm up and found herself looking at a large swarthy guy, his face partially covered with a black swimming mask. With one painful jerk he twisted Nancy's arm behind her back and reached for her other wrist. Just before he turned her all the way around, Nancy saw a large fraternity ring on his right hand.

Behind Nancy, Lori screamed. Nancy wrenched around for a second to see Lori being attacked by a second man. "No," she screamed. "No!"

Nancy went on the offensive then, delivering two powerful karate kicks to her attacker's knee joints. He cried out in pain but didn't loosen his viselike hold on her arms.

Lori had been more successful and wrenched herself free, taking off running down the beach.

Lori's attacker then turned his rage on Nancy. She felt the jarring pain of his fist against the side of her face and saw flashes of red and yellow light before sinking into unconsciousness!

Chapter

Five

Nᴀɴᴄʏ ᴡᴀs ꜰɪʀsᴛ aware of the cool sand against her back and head and the feeling of nausea in her stomach. Then, in one burst, she was fully awake and felt nothing but the pulsating pain along the side of her face and in her head.

Images swam in her head as she forced her mind to try to remember where she was. She could not will her eyes to open. The ocean, the beach, Lori Westerly, all that came floating back to her. Lori? Where was she? Hurt? Getting help?

Then one image took hold in her mind and forced out all the others—the image of a man's hand on her arm, and on that hand a ring.

Something about that ring, Nancy thought. Something about that ring . . . She shoved her pain aside, so she could concentrate on recapturing what that ring looked like. It was red. Ruby red. Two gold letters were on the stone, she remembered. Greek letters!

Nancy tried to focus only on her powers of concentration. If she didn't identify those letters now, she feared that they would be lost to her forever.

The Greek letter that looked like a triangular *E* and the capital letter *K* moved across her mind's eye. That would be Sigma Kappa.

And then suddenly Nancy became aware of another hand, this one gentle and holding her own. A voice quietly asked, "Nancy?"

Finally Nancy did open her eyes to look into those of Ira, who was kneeling next to her.

"Hello," Nancy said weakly.

"What happened, Nancy?" Ira asked. "Are you all right?"

Rolling over on her elbow to prepare to stand up, Nancy said only, "Two guys—" But a searing pain shot through her jaw, and she couldn't continue.

"Better come to my shop and get a cold cloth on that," he said, lifting her to her feet. "You can tell me about this there."

Nancy nodded and stood bent over, leaning on Ira for support. Just then Lori came sprinting down the beach toward them.

"Nancy, are you okay?" she called. Looking at Nancy's swollen face, Lori said, "Oh, no. They hurt you." Lori glanced quickly at Ira and then back at Nancy as she apologized, "I'm sorry I ran away, Nancy, but I thought I'd be of more use if I got help. But when I got up to the pier, I saw those two guys, still wearing their swim mask, running away," Lori explained. "So I turned around and came right back to you."

"You did the right thing," Nancy said, reassuring her. As she started to stand fully upright, she let out a loud groan. Her head was pounding.

"How badly are you hurt?" Lori asked with concern.

Nancy answered, "Not very. I'll live, I'm afraid. Oh, Lori, this is Ira."

"Hi, Ira," Lori said hastily, then turned again to Nancy. "I better take you back to the house to get something cold on that bruise."

"We can do that right over at the diving facility." Ira pointed to his building. "We were just going to head that way."

"Are you sure that's okay?" Lori questioned Nancy.

Nancy nodded. "Fine."

Hesitating, Lori asked, "Do you mind if I take that swim we were planning? I really have to swim every day, and as long as you'll be okay—"

"No problem," Nancy said. "I sure don't have two miles in me now. But I'll wait for you up there," she said, gesturing in the direction of Ira's shop.

Holding Ira's arm, Nancy tried to move without jarring her head. Even so, the pain was excruciating. When they reached the repair shop, Ira helped Nancy down onto a chair, gave her a cool cloth and a warm blanket, then pulled up a chair to sit across from her. Nancy leaned her aching head against the wall.

"How do you feel?" Ira asked gently.

"Terrific, from the neck down," Nancy answered.

"I think maybe I should take you to the emergency room to let a doctor take a look at you."

"No thanks." Nancy moved her jaw, checking to see if she had full mobility. "I'm sure nothing's broken. Just a shock to my system. As long as I keep this on it and get some rest, I'll be fine."

"If you change your mind, let me know. It's no problem," Ira offered kindly. "How about something to drink? A soda? Juice?"

"Either," Nancy said as Ira went into the back room.

"What did you see?" Ira asked as he handed Nancy a paper cup full of apple juice and sat back down across from her.

"Not much," Nancy answered between sips. "Two guys, wearing swimmers' masks and trunks. Big and strong. One with dark, curly hair. Lori and I were just taking off our shorts and jackets—"

34

"That's Lori Westerly?" Ira asked, interrupting.

Nancy nodded.

"Rina talked about her a lot," Ira said quietly. "Rina was very attached to her. Sorry, go on."

"Out of the blue, these two guys appeared. They must have been following us, but we were totally unaware."

Ira looked upset. "So much violence on this beach!" Standing up, he said to Nancy, "I had told myself to stop thinking that Rina's death wasn't an accident, but after talking to you and Susan this morning, and now this"—Ira gestured to Nancy's face—"I'm ready to go to the police and insist they open the investigation again!"

Nancy wanted more time to investigate on her own, to live in the sorority, and to understand Rina's life. She knew that sometimes she could learn more undercover, from people her own age, than the police could.

As she sipped her apple juice, Nancy wanted to tell Ira the truth, but she kept quiet. Although he seemed very nice, and although she felt she could trust him, it was still too soon to know for certain. Ira was in a perfect position to tamper with someone's diving equipment. And what was he doing down at the beach just after Nancy had been attacked? Lucky coincidence, or something more sinister?

"Are you saying the two incidents are connected?" Nancy asked innocently.

"No," Ira answered, "I don't see how that could be. They were probably just tough kids, like Lori said. Kids who get their kicks out of terrorizing people." Ira tightened his hands into fists. "And nothing gets me madder."

Hoping Ira would drop his idea of calling in the police, Nancy said, "I'm sure that was it. They were just having 'fun.'"

But maybe not, she thought. Maybe they really were after her and Lori!

"Is there anyone," Nancy asked Lori as they drove back to the sorority house, "who might want to hurt you—for any reason?"

Her wet blond hair brushed straight back off her face, Lori shook her head.

"Not that I know of. I think we were just in the wrong place at the wrong time." Glancing quickly at Nancy, Lori said, "Should I ask you the same question? Anybody want to hurt you for any reason you know of?"

"Nobody even knows me here," Nancy answered.

"It looked like you knew that guy Ira. Didn't you?" Lori asked.

"Not really. Susan and I met him just this morning at the diving facility," Nancy answered.

"Oh." Lori parked her car back at the house. "There's random violence on every beach in the world," she said thoughtfully. "Friends of mine were on an empty beach in Thailand—on the other side of the globe—and got beat up terribly."

Seeing how important it was for Lori to believe the attack was not meant specifically for them, Nancy didn't disagree.

She gingerly got out of the car, holding her aching head steady. Whatever dangerous thing Rina knew, Nancy thought, it's possible that Lori knows it, too. Nancy glanced over at Lori. And if someone wanted Rina Charles dead, then maybe Lori Westerly would be the next victim!

Chapter

Six

"OH, NANCY, I'M so glad you're okay!" Susan jumped up as Nancy entered her room. "Ira called and told me what happened. How do you feel?"

Nancy touched her bruised jaw. "A little tender, but fine otherwise," she said, and flopped down on her bed, without mentioning the dizziness and headache she also felt.

After Nancy described the surprise attack, Susan asked, "What do you think, Nan? Was this connected in any way to what we know?"

"That's the question I've been asking myself, too," Nancy said, staring at one of Rina's remarkable underwater photographs. "Is Lori

Westerly next on somebody's hit list? Or . . . ?"
Nancy rolled onto her side to try to get more
comfortable.

"Or what?" Susan asked.

"Or has someone *already* figured out that I'm a
detective, and what I'm after?"

Susan looked frightened.

"Lori believes that it was just random violence," Nancy said. "The kind that can happen
anywhere."

"It can," Susan agreed. "And I suppose that's
the most likely answer." Looking down at her
friend, she said, "But I bet you don't buy it."

Nancy smiled up at her. "Not yet," she said.

Susan said, "I'll be quiet now and let you get
some rest." But before she left the room, Susan
added, "Oh, just one more thing. When Ira
called, he asked if you and I would like to go out
Wednesday night with him and a friend of his.
He said he felt bad that you'd gotten such an
awful welcome to San Diego—and thinks you
need some fun."

Still smiling, Nancy said, "You like Ira, don't
you?"

"I guess you don't have to be a detective to see
that," Susan replied with a grin.

"So you want to go out with them Wednesday
night?" Nancy asked her friend.

"I'd love it. Will you come?"

"I'm not sure how Ned would feel."

"It's not a real date," Susan said. "Just think

that you're my chaperon. Ned would have to understand that."

Nancy laughed as she cautiously rolled onto her back. "Okay, okay. You've convinced me. I'll join you."

"Did Rina drive her own car to the beach that day?" Nancy asked Susan the next morning as they sat on the floor sorting through Rina's possessions and putting them in boxes.

"Yes. It was found on the highway near the beach. I drove down with Debbie and we brought it back here.

"It might be nice if we packed everything before tonight," Susan suggested. "Mrs. Charles said that she and her son would be here early tomorrow to pick up the car, along with Rina's other stuff."

"Yes," Nancy agreed. "The less they have to do, the better. This can't be easy for them."

Susan shook her head as she folded clothes. Nancy was packing Rina's books and looking through her papers for any kind of a clue.

"What's this name?" Nancy asked. "Rina's doodled it over and over in the margin of her notebook."

"It looks like Peterson to me," Susan answered, examining the page.

"But it's in two different handwritings," Nancy explained. "Someone in her class could have written the name down for her, and then

Rina could have copied it. See, the second handwriting matches the rest of the notes. Do you know who Peterson is?"

"No idea," Susan answered.

Nancy made a mental note of the name and continued looking through Rina's things but found nothing except the usual notebooks and class materials.

"You know," Susan said, "I was hesitant to join this sorority."

"Why?" Nancy asked.

"I don't like it when some people are chosen and others are left out."

"What made you change your mind?" Nancy asked, putting a pile of books into a carton.

"Well, Delta Phi has the highest academic standing on campus. They really do emphasize good grades in this sorority," Susan explained.

"It seems as though they also emphasize good looks," Nancy said.

"I guess," Susan said, and smiled. Although Susan wore no makeup and had her hair cut in a short and easy style, she was still a beauty. Her light blue eyes and black hair were striking. "I think that's why Rina was feeling so low. She felt neither pretty enough nor smart enough to be a Delta Phi."

"She looks very attractive here," Nancy said, examining a photo of Rina sitting on the porch of the sorority house.

Folding a sweater, Susan walked around and

looked over Nancy's shoulder. "Rina wore thick glasses and was self-conscious about them. She always took them off for pictures. She had terrible astigmatism that contact lenses couldn't correct. Her glasses really did change her appearance. But I bet you won't find one picture of her with her glasses on."

"But wait," Nancy said. "Didn't I just see them here?" She walked to Rina's dresser and spotted the glasses, then she asked, "How many pairs did she own?"

"Two. She always kept an old pair in her top desk drawer," Susan answered. "Why?"

Swinging around, Nancy opened the desk, and there, in a gold case, was the extra pair.

"I assume she couldn't drive without them?" Nancy asked.

"Of course not—she had terrible vision. Why all the questions?" Susan asked, confused.

"One more, and I'll answer you. How did both pairs of glasses get here?" Nancy asked, holding up both of them. "Was one pair in her car when you picked it up?"

"No, they were right there on the—oh, no!"

Nancy nodded her head as she saw that Susan understood.

"So Rina didn't drive to the ocean that day!" Susan exclaimed.

"Exactly," agreed Nancy. "Ira said she wouldn't dive alone, and now we know for sure that someone else was with her when she went to the beach that day. Either that person drove Rina's car, or her car was taken to the beach at another time," Nancy explained.

"You mean she was dead before she even got there?" Susan asked, startled.

Nancy shook her head. "No, the coroner's report had to have said it was a drowning, or else the police wouldn't have closed the case." Nancy contemplated what she had just said. "But something strange was going on before Rina ever got to the water."

As she spoke, Nancy's eye caught sight of an envelope pushed halfway under the closed door.

Silently moving to the door, Nancy flung it open. The hallway was empty. She bent over and picked up the envelope as Susan asked, "What's that?"

"Wait a sec," Nancy said, stepping out into the hall to double-check. Before opening the envelope, she knocked on the door to Debbie and Patty's room.

Patty was buttoning her shirt as she answered it.

"Hi," Nancy said quickly. "Did you see or hear anybody in the hall just now?"

Patty shook her head and grabbed a pair of running shoes from her closet. "Late for class, again," she mumbled.

"Sorry to bother you," Nancy said.

"No problem," Patty said while tying her shoes. "I doubt if anyone's around—everyone's probably in class already. Susan's the only smart one, not taking classes before eleven o'clock in the morning."

Nancy left Patty to finish her frantic dressing.

"Nobody in the shower room," Susan reported as she came back into the room at the same time Nancy did. "Open it, Nan," Susan said.

Nancy closed their door and opened the sealed envelope.

The note, printed on computer paper, said:

> Just in case you were wondering,
> that attack *was* meant for you.
> Get out of here, Nancy Drew.

Chapter

Seven

WHO IN THIS house owns a computer?"
Nancy asked Susan.

Susan was staring at the note in Nancy's hand.
"Oh, Nancy! This is starting to get too dangerous."

Nancy repeated her question about the computer, and Susan tried to get her thoughts clear
enough to respond. "A couple of the seniors do,
but I don't really know them very well. How can
you be so cool and businesslike?" Susan asked.

"I've been threatened before," Nancy said,
trying to calm her friend. "But I've never been
scared off. Threats just make me more determined."

"Nancy, I'd blame myself forever if anything happened to you because of me. Do you think maybe we ought to drop this investigation?"

"Absolutely not! Now there's even more reason for following this case to the end," Nancy said. "But I'll need your help."

"You have it."

"Okay. Computers," Nancy said, reminding Susan.

"Yes. Well, there's a couple of seniors on this floor who have them, and down in the basement study hall there's one that's available to all of us."

Racing downstairs to the basement, Nancy quickly typed the message she had received on the sorority's word processor. The typeface on the printout she made was identical to that of the letter in her hand.

Dead end, Nancy thought. Anyone could have written this. Every person in the sorority has access to this machine.

At eleven-thirty Nancy, dressed in a pale pink cotton knit dress, rang the doorbell of the huge Sigma Kappa fraternity house.

"Well, hello!" a good-looking guy said, greeting her. "I sure hope I can help you."

"I hope so, too," Nancy said with a smile.

"Let me guess," he said. "You're looking for a date Saturday night. I'd love to, thank you!"

"No, not exactly." Nancy laughed and looked at his madras plaid shorts and white T-shirt.

"Well, my name is Mark. Welcome to Sigma Kappa," he said. "Come on in."

"Thanks. I'm Nancy Drew."

"I am free Saturday night," Mark said. "No kidding."

"Sorry, but I'll probably be back home by then. I'm just visiting my cousin for a few days."

"Where's home?" Mark asked.

"A town in the Midwest called River Heights."

"Well, that's a fine place for a date. I've never seen River Heights. Shall I meet you there Saturday night? About eight o'clock?"

"I've actually come to buy a fraternity ring for my boyfriend," Nancy said, thinking that would discourage Mark. "He's a Sigma Kappa at Emerson College, and I wanted to give it to him as a gift."

"Is there a chapter at Emerson?" Mark asked. "I didn't know that. Anyway, dump him," he said with a grin. "He's not good enough for you."

As Mark and Nancy joked in the hallway, several of Mark's fraternity brothers passed them. Nancy kept an eye out for a large guy with dark curly hair, the one with the Sigma Kappa ring. She was less clear about what the other guy looked like, but they would both recognize her, she knew, so she was watchful for any unusual reaction.

"Could I see a brochure of your fraternity jewelry?" Nancy asked Mark.

"Sure. I can get it for you, but I was just going in to lunch. Want to join us? Your boyfriend can't object to that."

"I'm happy to join you," Nancy said.

"Now, that's what I like to hear!" Mark said.

Sigma Kappa fraternity house was not nearly so nice as the Delta Phi's. The dining room was loud and pretty messy. Nancy accepted a plate of macaroni and cheese that one of the fraternity brothers served her.

Everyone, it seemed, was looking at Nancy appreciatively. "You must be Mark's sister," someone said as he put his plate down on the table next to Nancy's. "I'm Jay."

"I'm Nancy," she said, shaking Jay's outstretched hand. "But not Mark's sister."

"Well, you're much too pretty to be his date," Jay said, sitting next to her. "You must be related somehow."

"Hey, hands off Ms. Drew," Mark said as other guys took seats at their table.

Nancy gave Mark a quick smile and turned back to the conversation. "I'm only visiting the school for a couple of days. I'm staying with my cousin at the Delta Phi house."

"Delta Phi," Jay said. "Beautiful, smart, and snobby."

"Especially smart," chimed in a man with the same dark, curly hair that Nancy identified with

48

her attacker. But his build was much too small. The other guy had been very large.

After finishing eating, Mark said, "Come on, let me get the jewelry information for you."

Leafing through the catalog, Nancy searched for the ring she had seen. "The one I was looking for has a red stone, like a ruby, in it, with Greek letters in gold. But I don't see it here."

"Nah. That hasn't been around for years. Too expensive. I think this one is the best." Mark pointed to a plain silver ring with Sigma Kappa embossed on it.

"But I saw someone wearing that ring just yesterday," Nancy complained.

"It must have been his old man's or something. He didn't get it here."

"Does anyone in this house have that ring?"

"Nobody," Mark said positively.

Nancy closed the catalog, disappointed to have another lead come to a dead end. "Well, thanks for your help, Mark, and for lunch, too."

"So I'll see you Saturday night?"

Nancy smiled. "Afraid not, but thanks anyway."

Nancy looked at the span of ocean she could see from the rooftop sun deck at the sorority house and thought about what direction to take with this frustrating case. There was one death already. And something is going on and certain people in this sorority know about it. But what is it, and who are they? Nancy had not begun to piece any of it together. Lori? Fran? Some of the girls in the inner circle? All of them? And outside the sorority who's involved? The men on the beach—who were they working with? Even Ira, Nancy had to suspect. Standing behind the white wooden railing high above the ground, lost in thought, Nancy barely heard the footsteps coming toward her.

All of a sudden Fran Kelly was next to Nancy. She took out a bright blue ribbon from her pocket and tied back her long straight hair.

Interesting, Nancy thought as she said hello. Is Fran following me, or is this a chance meeting?

"Hello," Fran answered, but said nothing more.

"Finished with your classes for the day?" Nancy asked, looking at her watch. It was three o'clock.

Fran nodded. "My Tuesday schedule is light. Monday, Wednesday, and Friday I suffer."

Nancy smiled. It seemed as though Fran was actually being a little friendly.

"I'm a math major," Fran said. "And I have a calculus test on Monday. But I've got too much on my mind to study."

Nancy waited patiently to see if Fran was going to say any more about herself. There were a couple of minutes of silence before Fran said, "As a matter of fact, *you're* one of the main things on my mind."

Fran's voice had changed completely. A hard, cold tone made her voice sound brittle. Her pretense of friendliness had vanished.

"Me?" Nancy asked, turning away from the ocean view to face Fran.

"Yes, you, Nancy Drew. You come here out of nowhere, and in one day you're driving off to the beach to go swimming with Lori Westerly," Fran said. There was no hiding the jealousy in her voice.

Nancy leaned back against the railing as she studied Fran Kelly.

"Just like your cousin's last roommate," Fran continued. "You remind me of her, you know that? Doing anything to get in with the right crowd."

Knowing that whatever she said would provoke Fran, Nancy remained silent—and on guard.

Now it was Fran who turned to face the ocean. She said, "But things are going to change around here for me—you just watch. Very soon I'm going to be an officer of this sorority."

Scanning the deck, Nancy saw that the only exit was the small stairway she had come up.

"My mother's best friend is the accountant for Delta Phi," Fran said, speaking slowly. "And she's just agreed to suggest me as the next treasurer."

So perhaps Fran will be next to know the dangerous secret that Rina knew. Looking at the angry girl in front of her, Nancy wondered if Fran would then be in danger.

"Yes, Lori should be getting a letter of recommendation from Linda Peterson very soon," Fran hissed.

Peterson? Nancy's breath caught. *Peterson* was the name written in the margin of Rina's notebook.

There was a frightening look in Fran's eyes as she began a tirade. "You're trying to do just what Rina did to me, Nancy Drew!"

As Fran's hands flew up from her sides, Nancy parried the attack she knew was coming. "So you'd better stop trying to push me out!" Fran shouted, shoving Nancy hard.

Nancy heard a loud crack as she felt the white wooden railing start to give!

Chapter

Eight

As THE RAILING gave, Nancy flung herself forward and fell into Fran. Immediately Nancy stood up and assumed the solid karate stance of a professional. Although she still knew nothing of Fran's motive, Nancy was ready to fight, if a fight was called for.

But Fran steadied herself, and took the violence no further. For an instant she looked shocked and frightened as she glanced over the edge of the roof to the hard concrete below. Without a backward glance, Fran turned and walked down the stairs.

As Nancy watched her go, she shook her head. Was Fran Kelly just a jealous, spoiled girl who went too far in trying to get what she wanted? Or, Nancy wondered, could this girl with the bright blue ribbon be a dangerous killer?

Nancy went downstairs then to Susan's room and called Ned. He answered the phone.

"Hey, Nance!" he greeted her.

"Oh, Ned, I'm so happy you're there. It's good to hear your voice!" Nancy said.

"It's always good to hear yours, but you don't sound so great right now. What's wrong?" Ned asked perceptively.

"I'm afraid this case is getting me down," Nancy explained.

"You need the old Nickerson pep talk?" Ned asked.

"Badly, and maybe some advice," Nancy said.

Conversations with Ned always helped Nancy sort out her thoughts. Often he, and Bess and George, would assist her on her cases. And right then Nancy was missing them. Susan, though a good friend, was no detective.

"I feel very far away and isolated," Nancy said softly, looking out the window of Susan's room as late-afternoon fog was rolling in off the ocean.

"Well, complaints about California I won't bother with," Ned said. "It's snowing here today, and you're probably lolling around in the sun."

"You're right." Nancy smiled into the phone, her spirits lifted just to be in contact with Ned. "The only problem with sunning is that I just nearly got pushed off a sun deck that's four flights off the ground."

Ned became serious. "Any other danger, Nancy? I hate it when you're working on a case that far away from me."

"Plenty. One threatening note, and an attack on a beach. But I'm fine." Nancy was quick to reassure him. "It's just that despite all this danger, I don't really have any concrete clues."

"Start from the beginning," Ned said to encourage her. Nancy briefly summarized the case.

"It must have been pretty important to someone to shut Rina Charles up," Ned said.

"Exactly," Nancy agreed.

"And *nobody* in that Sigma Kappa house has a ring like that?" Ned asked.

"Nope. Well, not according to Mark. Nothing's panned out. I don't feel there's anything to help me figure out who it was, or what Rina knew, or—wait," Nancy said abruptly. "The file box. There's a lead I haven't followed. Why didn't I think of that before?"

"What file box?" Ned asked.

"When Rina was made treasurer, she kept her paperwork in a file box. But Susan couldn't show it to me because Lori Westerly had already taken it from their room."

"Sounds like a good direction. But you'll need to figure out how to see it. You can't ask Lori."

"No. There's no way I can do that without

blowing my cover. I'll just have to figure out a way to get to that file box on my own."

"And I'm sure you will," Ned said with a worried sigh. "Nancy, please be careful. Remember this is a murder case. It sounds like one of those 'nice' college kids is dangerous and is going to try to make sure you *don't* find out what Rina knew. Also," Ned added gently, "one more word of caution, if you don't mind."

"What's that?" Nancy asked.

"Stay out of that Sigma Kappa house—I don't want you falling in love with any golden California Adonises."

"No chance of that." Nancy laughed. "I'm in love with an Emerson College student, whom I miss very much. I'll call soon," Nancy said as she and Ned kissed goodbye into their phones.

Sitting in the basement study hall after dinner, Nancy wrote a letter home to Hannah Gruen. Hannah had been Nancy's housekeeper, friend, and mother substitute since Nancy was three. Nancy had promised to write her a note from sunny California.

The only other person in the study hall at that time was Alice Clark, a quiet person whom Nancy knew almost nothing about, and who seemed to always be alone.

But within minutes Kathy, another member of Lori's crowd, came down the stairs and joined Nancy.

Opening her books, Kathy began to complain immediately. "I hate studying. I shouldn't be a student. I'm not cut out for it. Look at this junk," she said, pointing to a history text. "Who cares? I mean, really, I do not care one little bit whether something happened in 1066 A.D. or not."

"Are there any courses you enjoy?" Nancy asked.

"Music appreciation, I guess. But then, you have to listen to everything so carefully that it really takes the beauty out of the music. The other night after I'd been studying for a music test, I woke up in the middle of the night. There was a thunderstorm, and honestly, I lay there in bed trying to remember who the composer was before I figured out it was thunder!"

When Nancy began to laugh, Alice Clark looked up from her work and gave them both looks of annoyance. "Sorry," Nancy whispered.

"Let's get out of here," Kathy said in a normal voice. "Or are you in the middle of something you have to finish?"

"No, just a letter home," Nancy answered.

"Want to take a walk? It's warm and beautiful out there tonight." Glancing in Alice's direction, Kathy added, "It's too nice a night for even you to be studying, Alice. Want to come with us?"

"No, thank you," Alice said in a very quiet voice, and quickly looked back down at her book.

"I'd be glad to take a walk," Nancy said.

"Good, I'll meet you on the porch," Kathy said. "I'd better grab a jacket."

Nancy glanced down at the long-sleeved white shirt that she had borrowed from Susan and decided she'd be okay in just that.

"I swear, I don't know how that girl got into this sorority," Kathy said as soon as she and Nancy headed out into the clear, beautiful night. They both stopped for a minute and breathed in the fresh ocean air.

"I mean," Kathy continued, "she does *nothing* but study. She has no fun or friends. And it's not like she was a legacy or anything." Kathy tossed a light khaki jacket over her shoulders as she said, "Sometimes strange things happen in this place."

"Maybe she was asked to join to bring the sorority's grade point average even higher," Nancy said, glancing around at the buildings they were passing. SDU was a huge campus, and they were walking in a part of it that Nancy had not explored yet. "I know how Delta Phi values its high academic standing."

"Well, there are other methods for getting good grades besides studying," Kathy said meaningfully.

"Like what?" Nancy asked.

"Like 'cooperation,'" Kathy said with a smile. Walking past the large gymnasium and tennis courts, Kathy steered Nancy to the left. Kathy said, "In the biology building we've got a friend. A teaching assistant who's very cooperative."

"Cooperative?" Nancy asked innocently, knowing that Kathy was about to tell her something about cheating. Had Rina found out about this?

"And I was the one who made the contact," Kathy said proudly. "You know what I mean —he tells us what's going to be on an exam beforehand so we don't have to waste time studying the wrong things. In some of the departments we have contacts who will actually *give* us a copy of the exam beforehand. *That* kind of cooperative."

Nancy tried not to let her anger show. There's a lot going on in this prestigious sorority that isn't so impressive, she thought. And something that's very dangerous. And Rina Charles knew what it was.

"But *there*," Kathy said, pointing to the math building, "we have nobody. And me with a calculus test on Monday!"

"Is Fran Kelly in your class?" Nancy asked casually. "She told me she had a calculus test Monday, too."

"Same one," Kathy responded.

Nancy felt her heart pounding with the excitement of having discovered something useful —finally. This clever cheating scheme might well be the key to something more than just the high grade point average in Delta Phi.

"Has anyone ever gotten caught?" Nancy asked, pretending to care.

"No. Luckily for us. There could be big trouble for everyone if that happened. Big trouble." The talkative Kathy looked concerned. "I shouldn't have even told you, I guess. You *will* keep it to yourself?"

"Sure," Nancy said.

"Do you think you'll try to get in here?" Kathy asked Nancy as they continued their walk.

"I'm not sure," Nancy answered. "I think—". But before she could finish the sentence, she felt an intense pain in her right shoulder, a shooting pain so severe it took her breath away.

"What's wrong?" Kathy asked as Nancy moaned and reached back to the painful spot.

"Here—" was all Nancy could get out before she fell to her knees.

"Nancy!" Kathy screamed. "There's a dart in your back!"

Chapter
Nine

"PULL IT OUT," Nancy managed to say.

Feeling Kathy's hands hesitating, Nancy instructed her in a whisper, "Like a nurse with a syringe. Put two fingers flat on my back around the tip, and pull the dart with your other hand. Just get it out, please!"

Nancy felt relief immediately after Kathy removed the sharp object. Although her shoulder ached, she stood up and whispered, "We have to find out where that came from!"

"But you're bleeding, Nancy!" Kathy exclaimed.

"I'll be okay. Just listen. Shhh."

Nancy trained her ears to pick up any movement on the quiet campus. Nothing.

"Who would do such a thing?" Kathy asked as she and Nancy ran to look in the direction the dart would have come from.

"Nobody," Nancy said, feeling discouraged. A throbbing pain pulsed in her shoulder.

"He must have gotten away while we were getting this thing out!" Kathy said as she gave the blood-tipped dart to Nancy.

He? Nancy thought. Or perhaps *she?*

"You'd better get to the infirmary," Kathy said in a high-pitched voice. "It's not far—just beyond that group of buildings. Can you make it?"

Nancy nodded. "I may need a tetanus shot," she said.

"When do you think Mrs. Charles will get here?" Nancy asked Susan the next morning.

"I don't know," Susan answered as she quickly brushed her hair. "But I hope I don't miss them. I have to go to the library in a few minutes. I really have to study."

"I'll make sure I'm here when they arrive," Nancy said. "I'd like to meet them."

"How are you feeling this morning?" Susan asked Nancy.

"Fine," Nancy answered. "I slept like a log. But someone has definitely figured out that I'm a detective," Nancy said as she tried to move her sore arm. "What bothers me the most is that I don't know how they did it, or who they are."

Susan nodded. "Let's see how your back looks," she said, concerned.

Nancy delicately moved her nightshirt over her shoulder so Susan could look at her back.

"Your whole shoulder is turning colors," Susan reported. "Blue and red and purple."

"Now I'll really look like a dart board," Nancy said, joking. "At least I won't have to cover it with makeup, like my face."

"Oh, Nancy," Susan said seriously. "You're used to all this danger and can make fun of it, but I can't. What do you really make of all this?"

Nancy answered thoughtfully. "We are getting some information, at least. Rina may have been involved with this cheating ring, and wanted to tell the school authorities. Someone might have felt they had to get rid of her. Or," Nancy added, "the murder may have been related to something Rina learned while she was treasurer. Or maybe the two things are somehow connected."

"And suspects?" Susan asked.

"Well, cheating is one thing, and killing is quite another," Nancy answered. "A lot of people in this house may be involved in cheating. I wouldn't be surprised if the whole inner circle was involved, and maybe Fran, too. It still doesn't tell me anything about murder."

Susan picked up the red-and-green-striped

dart that lay on top of the dresser. It was about six inches long and had a needle-sharp point. "You have *no* idea where it came from?" she asked.

"None at all," Nancy said. "The area was silent and deserted by the time we looked around. The person who threw it had time to get away while Kathy was pulling that out of my shoulder," Nancy explained.

Susan winced at the description.

Nancy began to do gentle stretches and yoga postures. "I need to see that file box," she said. "Today."

"And today is your third day here. I spoke to Lori last night and asked her if you could stay a few more days. She said she'd let me know today."

"Okay," Nancy said, bending over to touch her toes.

"And tonight's our date with Ira and his friend," Susan reminded Nancy. "Are you sure you feel up to it?"

"Sure," Nancy said, standing up straight.

Susan began gathering up her books to go to the library. "One more thing you might be interested in. This afternoon at four o'clock is a big swim meet. Lori's diving, so everyone in the sorority will be there to cheer her on."

"Everyone will be out of the sorority house?" Nancy asked.

"Probably," Susan answered. "Why?" As she

placed her hand on the doorknob, Susan turned back to look at Nancy. "The file box?" she asked.

"Let's hope so. See you later."

Soon after Nancy was showered and dressed, Rina's mother and brother, Gary, appeared. Nancy introduced herself to Mrs. Charles as Susan's cousin, *not* as the detective investigating her daughter's death. Gary, Nancy noted, wore the same thick glasses that Rina had.

"You girls have all been so kind," Mrs. Charles said as she sat at Rina's old desk and looked at all the things that Susan and Nancy had packed. Gary began carrying things down to the car, and although Nancy wanted to help him, she felt it was important to sit and visit with Mrs. Charles for a while. There may even be a clue, Nancy thought.

"It meant so much to Rina that she was asked to be a Delta Phi—and so much to me," Mrs. Charles said. "And to think she was so quickly given a position of responsibility," she added with a sigh. "Do you know, my alumnae check came back endorsed by my own daughter." Rina's mother smiled proudly. "I gave twice my usual amount this year—in appreciation—six hundred dollars. I think Rina was very happy that I had been so generous. She thanked me every time we talked."

"Did anyone else endorse that check, Mrs. Charles?" Nancy asked, taking a guess that there would be two signatures needed for any sorority financial transaction.

Mrs. Charles nodded. She looked tired, and sad, as she answered, "Yes. That lovely young woman who was so upset at Rina's funeral —Lori Westerly."

Just then, there was a knock on the open door, and framed in the doorway was Lori Westerly.

Mrs. Charles stood up to embrace Lori, and they greeted each other warmly. "I heard you were here," Lori said as Gary returned to the room to get more boxes to carry downstairs. "I thought I might be able to help."

As Lori grabbed an armful of Rina's things, she turned to Nancy and said, "I got approval for you to stay a few more days. Susan said you'd like to."

"Thanks very much," Nancy said. "I really appreciate it."

"Oh." Mrs. Charles sighed. "There's nothing like Delta Phi for wonderful girls."

In the late afternoon the entire sorority house was empty. It was unnaturally quiet, without the usual buzz and drone of radios, hair dryers, and voices.

With a credit card Nancy expertly pried open the lock on Lori Westerly's door and silently closed it behind her.

Susan had told Nancy that the third floor had the most desirable rooms, and Nancy could see why. From Lori's window she had a breathtaking view of the water, beaches, and palm trees. Evidently, the higher you are in this sorority, Nancy thought, the higher your room is in the house. Nancy scanned the large room. Piled on the bed were clothes, books, and even a pair of swim fins. The desk was also disorganized. On the walls were posters of athletes. All divers, and all Olympic champions.

In the large walk-in closet Nancy found more athletic equipment. Lori's weights for working out, a wet suit for scuba diving, and also rock-climbing equipment. But not what Nancy hoped she would find.

Not until she lay down on the floor and looked under the bed did Nancy find the green file box Susan had told her about. Excitedly, she pulled it out, picked the lock, and looked in. But after examining the contents, Nancy felt disappointed. There was just a form letter thanking people who had donated money to Delta Phi and a listing of all the alumnae who had done so since the beginning of the school year.

How could this be worth anything? Nancy wondered. But then she remembered that Lori had felt it was important enough to retrieve before people even knew what had happened to Rina. Nancy took a small pad out of her pocket and quickly copied down the information. It may be nothing, she thought. But it's worth examining further.

Nancy relocked the file box, returned it to its exact place under the bed, and checked to make certain that everything in the closet was as it had been when she entered. She listened at the door before she swiftly and cautiously left Lori's room.

"Oh, good, you made it!" Susan exclaimed as she moved over to make room for Nancy on the bleachers in the huge indoor swimming arena.

In front of Susan sat Fran Kelly and Jan Miller. Looking back when Susan greeted Nancy, the two girls stopped the animated conversation they were having.

"The diving competition started about ten minutes ago," Susan said. "So far Lori has had one dive. She's getting ready for her second."

Jan Miller turned around once more.

"Hi," Nancy said as Jan stared directly at her.

But Jan didn't return the greeting. Strange, Nancy thought. She had been friendly enough on the porch the other day. It seems Fran Kelly may have been telling her some interesting things about me.

"Next diver, Lori Westerly, for SDU," came the announcement over the loudspeaker. "Double forward flip, with jackknife entry."

Lori approached the board with confidence, measured off her steps, and took a moment for deep concentration before she did the remarkable dive. Perfect entry, Nancy thought as she, along with the rest of the students sitting around her, burst into applause.

When Lori got out of the pool, she waved to her appreciative sorority sisters and then headed over to sit with another swimmer. He was a large guy who slipped his arm around Lori's shoulders affectionately.

"Is that her coach?" Nancy asked Susan.

"No. That's Mike Jamison. He's Lori's boyfriend—captain of the men's team; does breaststroke, butterfly, and men's relay."

Nancy looked over at Mike as Susan continued. "He's in Zeta Psi—pronounced Zeta 'Sigh,'" she said, joking and pointing to a row of young men who sat in the bleachers to their left. "Did you ever see so many muscles in one row? Those are his fraternity brothers. That's who we're having the Valentine's Day mixer with on Friday."

"I remember Lori mentioning the mixer at dinner the night I arrived," Nancy said, looking at Mike. Somewhere, she thought, I have met him. Nancy searched her memory as Mike put one leg in front of the other and bent down to stretch his calf muscles. His brownish blond hair was wet and slicked straight back on his head. Maybe just somewhere around campus the past couple of days. Or maybe . . . Nancy tried to recall somewhere else.

Nancy enjoyed the rest of the swim meet, and as everyone hurried out of the huge gymnasium afterward, Kathy walked up to her.

"Nancy, how are you doing?" she said in a high-pitched voice that was louder than Nancy liked.

"I'm fine now," Nancy said quietly. "Let's go out this exit," she suggested, leading Kathy and Susan away from the crowd.

To Susan, Kathy continued, "It was awful. There was a dart—*this long,* I swear!" Holding up her fingers to indicate the size, Kathy made it at least twice the length of the actual dart that Susan had already seen. "And it came out of nowhere!" Kathy exclaimed.

Nancy had successfully steered them away from the other students. The fewer people who knew about her incident, the better.

Kathy turned to Nancy. "Do you think we should have reported it after all?"

Nancy shook her head. "I'm sure it was just a mean prank," she said. To bring in the police would make her attacker go into hiding, and Nancy didn't want that. So they had told the nurse that there was no need to report it to campus security, and the woman hadn't seemed to care one way or the other.

"And I'm fine now, really, Kathy," Nancy said, smiling. "Thanks."

Kathy began to launch into the story again, making the dart another couple of inches longer, but Nancy cut her off. "I'd actually prefer it," Nancy said, "if you didn't tell anyone else about it—if you don't mind. Okay?"

Kathy looked disappointed. "Why not?" she asked.

"Because," Nancy explained, "sometimes when something like this happens, you get 'copy-cat' behavior." Nancy looked seriously at Kathy. "And I'd hate to have darts flying all over campus."

The muscles in Kathy's shoulders tightened. "Yeah, you're right," she agreed. "Gosh, I'm sorry. I just didn't think—"

Kathy turned around as a guy with wet hair and a bright smile tapped her on the shoulder. "Bob!" she chirped, smiling up at one of the divers. She said, "See you later," to Nancy and Susan and walked off with him.

Continuing their walk back to the sorority house, the two friends looked at each other. Susan put her hands about two feet apart and said, "*This* big, I swear!" They both burst into laughter.

"Do you think your black linen jacket would fit me?" Susan asked Nancy as they walked up the stairs to their room.

"Maybe. Why don't you try it on?"

"Were you going to wear it tonight?" Susan asked as she put the key in the door.

"No, you're welcome to borrow it," Nancy said, smiling. Susan, never one to pay much

71

attention to her clothes, was clearly excited about her date that night.

And Nancy had to admit to herself that after all the things that had happened the past couple of days, a pleasant evening out would be great.

Susan unlocked the door of their room and gasped. Then Nancy saw the dart that was piercing her pillow!

It was identical, except for the blue and yellow stripes, to the one that had jabbed her shoulder. This one was holding a piece of folded paper in place. Another message, Nancy knew.

You are trying very hard to find out what is none of your business. The last person who slept here knew too much. If you're smart, and I think you are, you'll give up *now*.

Chapter

Ten

"THEY'RE TERRORIZING YOU," Susan said, outraged.

"They're not succeeding," Nancy answered angrily, and tucked the blue- and yellow-striped dart into her suitcase, along with its mate.

"Well, I'm afraid they are with me, Nancy," Susan confessed, sitting on her bed and looking at the floor. "I'm very scared that something will happen to you." Looking up at Nancy, Susan said, "Please tell me your plans."

Nancy sat down across from Susan. "Tonight I plan to go out and have fun. That's my first plan. Tomorrow, I'm going to find out all I can about dart throwing and cheating on this campus. I wasn't able to get an appointment with the accountant, Linda Peterson, until Friday. But I do want to see what I can learn by looking at the financial records."

"Peterson? The name in the notebook?"

Nancy nodded.

"How did you find out who it was?" Susan asked.

"Fran Kelly generously told me."

Susan walked over to her closet and began choosing clothes for her date. "What role do you think Fran Kelly has in all this?" she asked.

"I don't know," Nancy admitted. "But she sure acts like she's got it in for me, so I need to watch her closely."

"She's so jealous," Susan said. "She could just be acting that way because she sees what an attractive and neat person you are."

"Or because she has something to hide," Nancy added. "Was there anything at all that you can possibly recall that Rina may have referred to about the cheating scheme?" she asked Susan.

"I spent all last night trying to think of that, and I have absolutely no memory of Rina giving me even a hint. If she was in on that, she was very closemouthed." Choosing a yellow sundress to wear under Nancy's jacket, Susan said, "Rina could keep a secret better than Kathy."

"Anyone could," Nancy said. "Unless Kathy was exaggerating the way they cheat like she did the story about the dart.

"I think," Nancy mused, "I'll have to learn more about this cheating ring before we know if that's related to Rina's murder."

"The chilis rellenos are great here," Ira said with a smile. "If you like them hot."

Nancy looked up from the menu in front of her and out the window to the waterfront. It was another clear, star-filled night in San Diego, and the ocean looked as if the stars were dancing on it wherever the lights from the Mexican restaurant reflected on its gentle ripples. A couple was strolling along the beach hand in hand, and Nancy found herself missing Ned more than ever.

"Nancy does, don't you, Nan?" Susan asked.

Nancy was so lost in thought that she hadn't heard Susan's question. "Don't I what?"

"Like hot food," Larry said. "This place is famous for its spicy food. If you order in English, they don't make it so hot, but if you order in Spanish, watch out." Ira's friend, Larry, seemed like a nice guy. He appeared to be studious in the wire-framed glasses he wore. Nancy smiled and told herself to stop thinking of Ned Nickerson for the moment and enjoy the evening.

As the waiter approached, Larry spoke to him in Spanish. Only a moment later the waiter returned carrying a platter of piping-hot nachos for everyone to share.

"I'm so glad you're okay now," Ira said kindly

to Nancy. "People don't usually get attacked on this beach, and I'm really sorry you were a victim on your first day in town."

Susan and Nancy exchanged glances, knowing full well that the attack on the beach had not been random. Far from it.

"Thanks," Nancy said to Ira. "I'm glad you showed up when you did. How did you happen to be there at that time?" Nancy asked curiously, still wondering whether she could trust Ira.

"He's a bit of a watchdog," Larry answered for his buddy. "Ira considers all the area within view of the Institute's scuba-diving resource center his own private beach."

"I wish that somehow I could have prevented what happened," Ira said.

"I wish I could have done something for Rina, too," Susan said.

As the waiter once again approached their table, Larry asked the group, "Trust me to order for us all?"

"Sure." Nancy smiled, and Susan and Ira nodded their agreement. Larry ordered in Spanish.

"But how could *you* have saved her?" Ira asked, looking at Susan. "You weren't around the beach that day, were you?"

Susan looked at Nancy, wondering whether she should tell him the truth. Nancy now felt certain that Ira really was trustworthy. She had been wrong before, of course, but this time she felt safe discussing the case with both Ira and Larry.

"Why don't you just explain what Rina told you before she died," Nancy suggested.

Susan nodded. "Right before she died, Rina confided in me that she knew something—a secret that she couldn't tell yet." Taking a sip of the ice water, Susan said, "We're afraid that someone wanted to make sure she never did tell it."

"Murder?" Larry asked, shocked.

"It's a possibility," Nancy answered.

"That makes more sense to me than what the police have come up with," Ira said thoughtfully. "Because there is *no way* that Rina Charles would dive with faulty equipment—or by herself."

A band began to play slow music in the background as they continued to talk.

"But murder?" Ira said. "She was such a nice kid."

Susan reached over toward Ira. Nancy saw Ira squeeze Susan's hand and felt glad that they liked each other so much.

For a few minutes the four of them sat in silence, until Ira turned to Susan and quietly asked her to dance. Nancy could see Susan's eyes light up.

When Susan and Ira left the table, Nancy asked Larry, "Did you say you were in the math department?"

Larry nodded and finished chewing a nacho before answering, "I work for Professor Zucker as a teaching assistant."

"Did you ever hear of TAs who 'cooperate' with students and give them exams beforehand?" Nancy asked.

"Sure," Larry answered. "But I wouldn't call it 'cooperating.' I'd call it 'cheating.'"

Nancy grinned. "Me, too." Taking a sip of her lemonade, Nancy asked, "How does it work?"

"Well, there's nothing tricky about how it works. Sometimes it's a straightforward bribe. And sometimes a good-looking girl finds a TA to fall in love with her, then she asks him to do her 'this one little favor'—to give her the test questions before the exam. He asks her to please never tell anyone that he's done it or he'll lose his assistantship, and she agrees. She then shares the exam with all of her friends who are taking the class, and they laugh behind his back. After they all ace the final, she breaks up with him. She has to find someone in another department to keep her average up. Nice, huh?"

"Not very," Nancy answered. "Why do people fall for it?"

"They probably don't more than once," Larry answered. "Now let me ask you a couple questions, okay?"

Before waiting for Nancy's agreement, Larry said, "Is it going on at the Delta Phi house?"

Nancy looked at Larry for a minute before deciding to nod.

"And you think this is what Rina knew? Why she was killed?"

Nancy shrugged. "Maybe."

"But would blowing the whistle be enough reason to knock her off?"

"Couldn't the consequences of being caught be very serious?" Nancy asked.

"Yes," Larry agreed. "But murder? Whew!"

Nancy glanced over at the dance floor and saw Susan and Ira heading back to the table, hand in hand. Great, Nancy thought. It's time something good happened to Susan!

As their waiter returned with plates of steaming food, Larry said, "Delta Phi has such a good reputation for high grades. Who would ever have thought it?"

Susan and Ira took their seats at the table just as Nancy said to Larry, "There's a calculus test Monday that some of the girls in this cheating ring have to take. They don't have a contact in the math department, though. Do you know anything about that exam?"

"Nope."

"Do you think you could write a phony calculus test?"

Larry tipped his glasses up and peered into Nancy's eyes. "I thought you'd never ask. I'd be delighted!"

"What's going on here?" Ira asked as he and Susan sat down.

"Chilis rellenos, enchiladas verdes, and chicken mole," Larry answered. "At your own risk."

"I mean about writing a phony exam?" Ira asked.

"After seven years of advanced mathematics, Nancy and I have finally discovered something practical I can do with it," Larry proclaimed as he began to serve himself an enchilada. "We are about to infiltrate a group of cheaters."

"You're going to give them a phony exam?" Susan asked nervously.

"Yes," Nancy answered. "And find out if there's more to this scheme than good grades."

"Like money involved?" Ira asked.

"Perhaps." Nancy nodded, serving herself some of the hot chilis rellenos. "It could be that Rina discovered something she wasn't supposed to discover. I want to know what that was, and I think I'm going to have to burn my candle at both ends to find out."

As the music became fast and loud, Susan asked, "How will getting in with them help?"

"I think," Nancy said, "that they're the only ones who can lead me to a murderer."

Chapter

Eleven

WHEN NANCY TAPPED gently on Kathy's door the next morning, a tired voice called out, "One minute."

"Sorry I woke you," Nancy said apologetically when Kathy opened the door in her pajamas, her long, frizzy hair sticking up in all directions.

"Oh, it's all right. It's eleven o'clock already. I should have been awake long ago." Kathy yawned. "I just stayed up late studying. Actually, I didn't *start* studying until late." Rubbing her eyes, Kathy said, "I wasn't cut out to be a student."

"I have something that may help that," Nancy proclaimed with her most winning smile.

"Well, come in," Kathy said with interest, and stood aside so Nancy could enter.

Inside, Nancy pulled a manila envelope from behind her back and presented it to Kathy.

"What's this?" Kathy asked, locking her door.

"Good news," Nancy said, "for calculus students."

"Oh, Nancy!" Kathy shrieked, taking the papers out of the envelope. "It's not!"

"It is!" Nancy said, feigning pride. "Monday's exam."

"How did you ever get it?" Kathy asked, wide-eyed.

"It was surprisingly easy," Nancy explained, and went into the story she had decided to tell. "I was looking around this morning when I began talking to this guy in the math department. I guess he's a teaching assistant. I asked him how difficult introductory calculus was, and he said, "Not very. Want to see a test we'll be giving soon?"

"Oh, no!" As Kathy squealed with delight and looked over the exam, Nancy thought about what Larry had said when they met on campus that morning. "The hardest part was making sure I didn't put anything on there that might actually show up on Monday's test," he had said with a grin.

"That jerk!" Kathy declared. "He just *gave* it to you?"

"Not exactly," Nancy said, trying to be a bit

vague. "Let's just say I borrowed it, with the help of a nearby copier when he got called out of the office."

Kathy looked impressed. "That's great. So he won't even know he's been 'cooperative.' That's the best! Thank you, Nancy," Kathy said, hugging the phony exam close to her. "Thank you so much."

Leaving Kathy's room, Nancy became aware of the time pressure she had just put herself under. Kathy, and anyone she shared the exam with, would know by Monday morning at nine o'clock that this one was a fake.

It's now Thursday, Nancy thought. By Monday morning I'd better have solved the mystery of Rina Charles's death!

Posted on the wall of the chapter room, next to the framed scholarship awards, was a listing of everyone's grade point average in the sorority. Let's see, thought Nancy as she searched through the names—Lori, Jan, Ellen, Pam, Johanna. Yes, almost all the inner circle have a four-point average. All except Kathy, and she's pretty close to it with a three-point-eight. Pretty good for someone who hates studying.

Alice Clark was the only other student with straight *A*'s, and there was no doubt in Nancy's mind that she deserved them.

Nancy was still looking at the list when Debbie wandered in. "Hello there," she said in her usual friendly manner. "Are you going to join us for the Valentine's party tomorrow?"

"Sure," Nancy answered.

"It should be fun. You examining our intellect?" Debbie asked.

"It's pretty impressive," Nancy answered. "So many high averages."

"Mine's not up as high as I wish," Debbie said. "And I want to get into graduate school in two years."

Looking at Debbie's name, Nancy saw that she had a three-point-two-five average. Surely respectable, but lower than many. What, Nancy wondered, did the people who didn't cheat know about what was going on?

"Well, I think I'll head upstairs. I've got a paper calling to me." Debbie sighed.

"I'll walk up with you," Nancy said.

When they reached Debbie's room, Nancy saw Patty in there working on something at her typewriter. Nancy had observed that the two of them worked very hard on their studies.

"Mind if I come in for a minute and ask you something?"

"Come on," Patty called out from her desk. "I need a break."

"Last night I was talking to this guy who's a grad student," Nancy said. "He told me he knew of an exam-stealing scheme that's going on in some of the sororities." Nancy spoke slowly and watched the girls' reactions. "He said that the authorities are getting wise to it and want to start prosecuting the students who are involved."

Patty pushed her glasses up and asked curiously, "How would anyone steal an exam?"

"Apparently," Nancy explained, noticing that Debbie had turned away and was looking at the books on her desk, "they don't have to be stolen, exactly. There are some helpful assistants that give them away."

"Well, if you see a political science one floating around," Patty said lightly, "pass it on—please."

"Do you think that ever goes on here?" Nancy asked.

Patty shrugged, put her glasses back on, and returned to her work. Debbie said, "I'd be shocked if it did."

But the blush in Debbie's fair skin led Nancy to believe that this was in no way shocking to her. While Nancy was convinced that Debbie wasn't part of the ring—her grades weren't as high as the others, nor as high as she wished they were —it appeared as though she knew of it.

"You've never heard anything about it?" Nancy asked.

"Listen," Debbie said abruptly, "that would be awful, a really awful thing to do to any TA." She shook her head angrily as she said, "After all those years of study and work, it could blow your career. It's horrible."

"I agree," Nancy said gently. As she left the room, she understood that Debbie knew about this scheme from the other end, from a TA who had been asked, or used.

"I'm a detective in training," Susan said as she burst into their room with a smile. After her date with Ira the night before, Susan was happier than Nancy had seen her since she arrived in California.

"What did you dig up?" Nancy asked, looking at the papers Susan was carrying.

"Only this," Susan said, handing her a list that was titled, "SDU, Clubs and Organizations." "I went to the Office of Student Affairs and got this list of athletic and social clubs." One was circled —"On Target." Susan excitedly read the description out loud, " 'Dart throwing for the beginner to the advanced.' "

"Susan Victors!" Nancy said, delighted. "This is great work!"

"And a little good luck, too," Susan said, pointing to the letters TH7BH that followed the description. "It meets tonight, Thursday, seven o'clock at Blake Hall."

"It's worth a try," Nancy said, smiling at Susan.

"I've saved you and your cousin a seat," Kathy said, greeting Nancy on the way into the dining room that evening. "Come join us at Lori's table."

As Nancy and Susan followed Kathy to the

table, Nancy was aware that Jan Miller was not sitting there, but was seated across the room with Fran Kelly. This should be interesting, Nancy thought.

"I'm so glad I got a chance to see you dive yesterday," Nancy said to Lori, who was seated right beside her. "You were wonderful."

"Thanks. The back flip nearly landed me in the bleachers, but otherwise I felt okay about it."

Nancy smiled. "More than okay," she said encouragingly. "Excellent. And the judges seemed to think so, too."

"What do you guys think about Jeff Arthurs?" Johanna asked everyone at the table. "Pretty cute, huh?"

"Are you going after him at tomorrow's mixer?" Ellen asked.

Johanna nodded and asked Lori, "Is he going with anyone?"

"As far as I know, he's fair game," Lori answered.

"Go for it," Kathy said.

While the rest of the girls at the table were talking together, Lori turned to Nancy. "I heard you had another accident," she said quietly.

"Accident?" Nancy asked.

Lori nodded as she chewed on a piece of fried chicken. "With a dart."

"Oh, yes," Nancy said, buttering a biscuit. She glanced at Kathy, who was chatting with Susan. "It's actually not looking very accidental now."

"I agree," Lori said. "When Kathy told me about it, I really started to wonder. Two attacks in one week is pretty outrageous. Do you have any idea what it's about?"

"None," Nancy said, shaking her head. "None at all."

"Do you know anyone in town who'd want to hurt you?"

"I don't know anybody in town at all," Nancy said. "Or at least I didn't before I arrived four days ago."

After their conversation, Lori stood up, tapped on her water glass, and made the usual evening announcements.

As they all filed out of the dining hall, it was no surprise to Nancy that Fran Kelly and Jan Miller approached her. Jan's short, straight hair framed her smiling face as she said sarcastically, "I'm *so* glad Lori found herself another puppy." She turned her back to Nancy and shot over her shoulder, "She was lonely when the last one died, poor thing."

Hearing Fran's laughter, Nancy turned to face her. As Jan walked away, Fran stopped laughing. In hushed tones, her mouth close to Nancy's ear, she said, "Your cousin's *last* roommate didn't end up so great when she got the special treatment, now, did she?"

Chapter
Twelve

N<small>O, SHE DIDN'T</small>, Fran," Nancy said angrily. "Rina Charles ended up dead." The two of them were standing on the back stairway, and Nancy decided it was time for the direct approach with Fran. "And just what do *you* know about that death?"

"I know," Fran said, with a hint of a smile on her face, "that the fool went scuba diving with faulty equipment. Everyone knows that. The police have confirmed it." Fran took a step up and looked down at Nancy. "Do you really think you are smarter than they are, Nancy Drew?"

Nancy passed her and turned sideways to

block Fran's way. "I don't know what the police learned," Nancy said. "But let me ask a question that I bet they didn't ask. Where were *you* when it happened?"

"When Rina died?"

Nancy only nodded, still blocking her way.

"How do I know where I was?" Fran answered, glaring at Nancy. "That's something the police didn't ask any of us, because they were smart enough to know we couldn't answer it. Nobody knows *when* Rina Charles died. Nobody knows when she put on that wet suit and weight belt and jumped into the Pacific Ocean."

Nancy was aware that absolutely nothing in Fran's manner suggested discomfort at the question. Fran's voice had been unwavering, and she had looked directly at Nancy as she spoke.

Fran then added coldly, "Rina wasn't the kind of person you'd miss just because she was gone for a day."

Either this person is innocent, Nancy thought, stepping aside, or she's a very fine liar. But if Fran doesn't have anything to do with Rina's death, then why is she behaving so cruelly toward me? Nancy wondered.

On the second floor, Nancy headed toward Kathy's room. She had more questions to ask, and now was the time to start asking them.

Kathy's door was open, and when she saw Nancy in the hall, she called out, "Come on in!

I've got plenty of time to visit now—thanks to you!"

Kathy was looking in the mirror above her dresser and applying eye makeup to her large green eyes.

Nancy gently closed the door behind her before she asked, "Do you remember if you mentioned to anyone that you and I were going for a walk the other night before we went out?"

Kathy licked the tip of her eyeliner pencil and mumbled, "Didn't we leave from the study hall?"

"No," Nancy said, reminding her. "Remember, you needed your jacket"—Nancy gestured to the khaki jacket that Kathy had worn—"and went upstairs to get it first."

"Oh, right," Kathy answered, her eyes open wide as she brushed mascara on her lashes.

"Did you tell anyone then?" Nancy asked.

"Nope," Kathy mumbled, concentrating on her eyes.

Kathy turned and smiled at Nancy. "Lori was very pleased with your helping Delta Phi out, by the way. I told her about that, and she thinks you're great."

"You're all very welcome." Nancy touched the collar of the jacket as she asked the next question. "Does everyone in the sorority know about the teaching assistants that help you out?"

"Are you *kidding?*" Kathy exclaimed. "Only a

few of the very special sisters, if you know what I mean." After she rubbed some lip gloss on her mouth, Kathy added, "I actually should never have told you; I don't know what made me do it. But I'm glad I did!" She smiled. "Maybe I'm psychic or something."

"Was Rina one of the special ones?" Nancy asked.

"Rina Charles? No way!" Kathy ran her fingers through her long curls, pushing them into an order of sorts as she said, "Rina was *not* one of the special people." Kathy hesitated. "I hate to say it, but I never really understood why she and Lori were close. Rina was nice, but, I don't know, she just didn't seem the right type. Anyway," Kathy added, "*I'm* in charge of the exam 'borrowing,' and if anyone was let in on the secret, I'd know." Curious, Kathy added, "How come you asked?"

"Just wondering about the sorority, I guess, and how it works," Nancy answered as casually as possible. If Kathy is right and Rina did *not* know about this, Nancy thought, then this path leads me to another dead end. Then, Nancy thought, this phony exam scheme has been pointless. It won't get me any closer to the killer, and it may get the killer closer to me.

"Well, I wouldn't be worried about getting in if I were you," Kathy said reassuringly as she touched Nancy's shoulder. "If you decide to come to SDU, I'm sure there'll be a place for you in Delta Phi." Looking at her watch, Kathy said, "Meeting time. I'd better move it. We're electing a treasurer tonight!"

Blake Hall was well lit, though empty, when Nancy reached it a little after seven. On the bulletin board, under Today's Activities, was listed "On Target—Room 207."

When Nancy walked into the room, all the desks were moved aside and four dart boards were set up against the wall. Only about seven people were in the room, all guys. Nancy had never seen any of them before.

She stood for a moment at the door, surveying the situation.

"Don't be shy," a voice called out. "We're always short on girls."

Nancy walked over to the person who issued the invitation. "Actually darts isn't my game," she replied. "I was just looking for some friends."

"Male or female?" he asked, picking up three more darts.

"Female," Nancy answered, taking a stab at it. "I think they usually come here on Thursday nights."

He threw a straight powerful shot at the target as Nancy asked, "Do you have a list of your members?" He picked up another dart, closed one eye, and aimed.

"Nope. We're not that organized," he an-

swered, picking up another dart, closing one eye
and aiming. "Whoever comes is welcome, usually only about six of us show up. Darts isn't a big
sport on campus." His last dart missed the
target, hit the edge, and fell to the floor.

"Well, you do your best," he said good-
naturedly. "Sometimes you get a hit and sometimes you get a miss."

Nancy smiled as she watched him throw his
last shot. It hit the center of the target, directly in
the bull's-eye.

"Nice!" she said appreciatively.

"Thanks. Sure you don't want to try?"

"Not right now, thanks. Do you ever have any
girls come?" Nancy asked.

"A couple show up every once in a while," he
answered. Then he made note of his score on a
piece of paper and called, "Jonathan, you're on."

"Do you know their names?" Nancy asked.

"I wasn't here last week, but someone said a
girl showed up then."

"Do you know who she was?" Nancy inquired.

"Nope, and most of these guys wouldn't know
a pretty girl from a dog. They're really into
darts."

Turning to Nancy, he said, "Sorry I can't be
more helpful. I don't have any idea if your
friends ever come here. We're pretty loose about
that kind of thing."

"Sure," Nancy answered, discouraged.
"Thanks anyway."

Well, she thought to herself as she left Blake Hall. You do your best. Sometimes you get a hit, and sometimes you get a miss.

This time, as Nancy walked across campus in the dark, she kept alert, watching for people, darts, or anything else.

After the meeting, when Susan came back to her room, she found Nancy lying on the bed thinking about the case.

"Who got it?" Nancy asked curiously, putting her thoughts aside for the moment.

Susan shrugged her shoulders as she reported, "Alice Clark is our new treasurer."

"Alice Clark?" Nancy asked. "That's a surprise!"

"To you and everyone clse," Susan said. "A lot of people really wanted that job. And, of course, Fran Kelly had her heart set on it. She even read a letter from our accountant, Linda Peterson, saying she'd be the best. It was sort of pathetic," Susan added.

"And Alice?"

Sitting beside Nancy, Susan said, "Alice was silent, as always. She didn't give a speech, like the others did, or say anything about how she was qualified for the position—only kind of a shy 'thank you' after she was elected."

Susan took her shoes off and crossed her legs under her. "Lori Westerly spoke for Alice, saying that Alice was the most brilliant person around, stuff like that. It was obvious that Lori wanted Alice to be treasurer, and that's all you need around here, I guess." Susan sighed. "Why do *you* look so discouraged?" she asked.

"Every time I think I'm getting somewhere, I run into a dead end," Nancy explained to her friend.

"Kathy says that there's no way Rina could have known about the exam stealing." Nancy leaned her head back against the wall and thought out loud. "But if Kathy knows that Rina was murdered, and that her involvement in the cheating scheme was the cause of her death, then of course Kathy never would have told me that Rina was involved."

Looking back at Susan, Nancy continued, "So either Kathy is an excellent liar, or she was telling me the truth, and cheating has nothing to do with why Rina was killed."

"Which do you think?" Susan asked.

"I think Kathy is telling the truth," Nancy said, folding her arms across her chest. "And that I've set up a group of people to study a phony exam for Monday who have nothing to do with the murder."

Susan rested her elbows on her knees, and looked down.

"Tomorrow, though, I can finally get into Peterson's office—maybe there I'll find the information we need," Nancy said, trying to sound hopeful.

"What about Fran Kelly and Jan Miller?" Susan asked. "They've been so cruel to you."

Nancy shook her head. "I'm starting to think that's just Fran's nature—she's jealous—and somehow she convinced Jan not to like me." Nancy crossed her outstretched legs at the ankles. "Maybe all these aggressive people are a smokescreen, keeping me from seeing someone not so obvious."

Susan looked at Nancy's determined face as Nancy continued, "Someone who could be in the background. Someone," Nancy said, "like Alice Clark."

"Where are you going now?" Susan asked as Nancy got up from the bed and pulled a bright purple sweatshirt over her short-sleeved shirt.

"Down to the study hall," Nancy replied with a smile.

Alice Clark was sitting—just as Nancy thought she would be—in her regular seat at one of the long tables.

"Congratulations," Nancy said out loud, since they were the only two people there.

Alice looked up from the large book in front of her, which Nancy noticed had diagrams of the human skeleton. "Thanks," she said, putting the top on her yellow pen.

"Anatomy?" Nancy asked, standing next to Alice.

"Physiology," Alice said.

Alice's answers were always only one word. Nancy wondered if it was going to be possible to get into a more extended conversation with this very private person.

"Do you mostly study science?" Nancy asked.

"I'm premed." Alice nodded.

"That must be time-consuming," Nancy said, sitting down across from Alice.

"I like it," Alice said. Leafing through her physiology book, she found a page that showed a large drawing of the musculature system. "See these points?" she asked Nancy, pointing to two spots in the neck. "If you press exactly *there,* you can make a person pass out cold."

"Did you learn that in physiology?" Nancy asked innocently as Alice slowly closed the book. Nancy knew very well about the pressure points in the neck.

"In judo," Alice answered, looking directly at Nancy.

"I study karate," Nancy said, meeting Alice's gaze.

"I wondered," Alice said as two freshman walked into the study hall laughing. Seeing Nancy and Alice, they lowered their voices and put their books down on the back table.

Alice took the top off her highlighting pen and once again began reading the text in front of her.

"See you later," Nancy said, standing up.

As she headed back up the stairs, Nancy tried to sort out what she had just learned. Alice was telling her something, she knew, something important about those pressure points.

Was she describing to Nancy how Rina Charles was killed? Was Rina unconscious before she was thrown into the ocean? And if that was the case, how did Alice know it?

Was this a warning of some sort? Nancy wondered. Was the quiet, unassuming Alice Clark a murderer?

Chapter

Thirteen

IN HONOR OF Valentine's Day, Nancy put a red belt on over her denim dress and folded a white lace hanky into her breast pocket when she dressed on Friday morning.

She had not sent Ned a card, and the two-hour time difference made it too late to call him. He'd be in class already. But tonight, Nancy thought, smiling at the picture of Ned she had taken from her wallet, I will call my number-one valentine.

Putting the photograph away and looking in the mirror, Nancy brushed her hair and then picked up the car keys Susan had left for her. It was only eight-thirty in the morning and Susan was still sleeping.

Nancy avoided the dining hall and hurried outside to head to the accounting offices at 4846 Thirty-fifth Street.

Counting on the likelihood that nobody had let the accountant know yet about the election of Alice Clark, Nancy told the receptionist that she was the interim treasurer of Delta Phi and had come to see the sorority's records.

"Ah yes," said the older woman at the desk. "Ms. Peterson told me you'd be here. Come right this way. I'm Mrs. Haft, and I'll be glad to help you."

"Thank you so much," Nancy said. She followed the receptionist around to a file cabinet, and as she looked through folders, Mrs. Haft asked Nancy, "Did you bring this month's bookkeeping, dear?"

"No, I'm sorry," Nancy answered. "We're just getting things organized again, since the tragedy."

"Wasn't that terrible?" the kind woman said. "To have that happen to a fine, bright girl like Rina." Shaking her head, Mrs. Haft said, "I always warn my kids about the ocean. You just can't trust it." She gave several folders to Nancy as she added, "Not that they listen." Then she made a beeline to the front desk to catch a ringing phone.

After about thirty minutes of studying the sorority's financial situation, Nancy was about to quit. Nothing looked the least bit suspicious.

Rina, and the treasurers before her, had been well organized and meticulous. And Nancy had no doubt that Alice Clark would be the same.

But as Nancy was about to give up, something caught her attention. Under the page marked "Alumnae Donations," Nancy had scanned down to the name Marsha Charles. There beside Rina's mother's name was listed the amount of one hundred and fifty dollars. Nancy's heart began to race as though she had just finished the fifty-yard dash. Nancy was certain that Mrs. Charles had told her that she had donated six hundred dollars this year.

"Finally," she said under her breath.

"What's that?" Mrs. Haft asked, walking by Nancy at that moment.

"Oh, nothing." Nancy smiled, trying to hide her excitement. "I'll just need to reproduce some of this, please."

"Right over here, dear," Mrs. Haft said.

As Nancy carefully ran the papers through the copy machine, she tried to be cautious about her discovery. It's possible that this is only a book-keeping error, she warned herself.

But her heart wouldn't stop racing, because Nancy knew that it was also possible she had finally found a major clue.

When Nancy arrived back at the sorority house, Susan had already left for her classes.

Locking the door behind her, Nancy sat down

at Rina's old desk, took out the list of alumnae donations from the accountant's office, and found the information she had copied from the secret file box. Quickly scanning her notes, she looked for the evidence she needed.

There it was! Nancy let out a deep sigh, unaware that she had been holding her breath. Next to Marsha Charles's name was listed the amount she had actually donated—six hundred dollars.

Here was a lead. A concrete lead. The embezzlement of money—maybe a lot of money—and a reason for murder.

A knock on the door startled Nancy, and she quickly put away her paperwork as she called out, "One minute." But before she could stand up, she heard a key in the door and Susan walked in.

Nancy jumped up, quickly closed the door behind Susan, relocked it, and said in an excited whisper, "We've got a missing piece to this puzzle!"

"Oh, Nancy, finally! Tell me," Susan pleaded.

"I'll show you," Nancy said, pulling the papers out of the top desk drawer.

"See this?" Nancy asked, pointing to the sheet she had copied. "This is a listing of all your alumnae donations. It totals ten thousand dollars this year."

"Pretty generous," Susan said, looking at the sheet. "Why is it the missing puzzle piece, though?"

"Because *this*," Nancy explained, pointing to the handwritten list she had copied from the file box, "is the *true* amount that was given. I haven't added it up yet, but look at all these discrepancies." Her pencil tip ran back and forth. "This person gave one hundred fifty dollars, and the amount submitted to the accountant was twenty-five. And here—"

"And the difference?" Susan said, interrupting Nancy and speaking rapidly. "Who has the money? Did Rina—"

"We don't know. Maybe Rina was in on it, but more likely, she just discovered it and was about to blow the whistle."

As Nancy reached over to Susan's desk and picked up a calculator, Susan asked, "I wonder why they kept this list of the real contributions."

"So they could write the contributors thank-you letters for the actual amounts. Only the amount they reported in the official records was a whole lot less. Let's figure out how much less," Nancy said.

As Nancy called off the differences to Susan, Susan added up the totals.

In only a few minutes Susan had the total. "Fifteen thousand dollars less!" She gasped. "This *must* be it, Nan, this must be what Rina knew."

"Yes." Nancy sighed. "Maybe nobody would commit murder for a better grade, but I'm afraid someone would to keep from being exposed as a thief."

"Lori?" Susan asked.

"She surely knows about the embezzlement," Nancy said.

"And maybe this is the reason that Fran Kelly was so desperate to be treasurer," Susan continued. "And maybe Alice Clark knows now, and—"

"Just because we have this one puzzle piece doesn't mean we know who did it," Nancy explained. "We're no closer to the murderer. We just have a reason."

Susan nodded and jumped as someone knocked at the door just then.

"One minute," Susan called out, and quickly glanced at Nancy.

Nancy put away all the paperwork and took out an SDU catalog before she went to the door.

"I just wanted to make sure you were coming to the party this afternoon," Lori said as Nancy opened the door. "There's a friend of Mike's coming that I think you'll like. And I'm *sure* he'll like you; I told him about you already."

Nancy stood at the door talking to Lori as Susan busied herself cleaning up a pile of clothes on her bed. "I don't know," Nancy confessed, "I really miss my boyfriend today. I was just going to call him and tell him I'll be back home soon."

"I'm sorry to hear that. You really are welcome

to stay longer, you know," Lori said. It was hard for Nancy to believe that this warm person knew all about the embezzling.

"Thank you," Nancy said, still standing in the doorway.

"My friend's name is Peter," Lori said, backing up, "He's very cute!"

"Thanks." Nancy smiled. "See you down there later."

"What is it?" Susan asked Nancy when she saw her leaning against the closed door, the color drained from her face.

"Lori's jacket," Nancy answered when she was certain that Lori's footsteps were far away.

"What about it?" Susan asked.

"It's the one that Kathy was wearing the night I got hit with the dart."

Chapter

Fourteen

So what if she's wearing Kathy's jacket?" Susan asked curiously. "Everyone borrows clothes around here."

Nancy shook her head and tiptoed away from the door to speak. "I don't think it's Kathy's," she said. "I think it's Lori's."

Susan was even more confused. "I don't get it, Nan."

"It's a lot of guesses," Nancy admitted, speaking quickly and quietly. "But I think I'm on to something. Listen." Nancy sat back down on the desk chair to explain to Susan. "I think that when Kathy went upstairs to get something warm to put on Tuesday night she ran into Lori, who had perhaps just come in. Kathy told her she was going for a walk with me and asked if she could borrow her jacket."

"So Lori knew you were going on the walk?" Susan asked. "And she followed you, and threw a green- and red-striped dart into your shoulder?"

Nancy nodded. "It's a possibility," she said.

"You think Kathy is innocent?" Susan asked.

"I do. She was so shocked by it all. And I just don't think she'd be able to act that well." Nancy shrugged. "But I've been wrong before, so I'll just keep watching."

Opening the desk drawer where Nancy had put the embezzlement information, she and Susan looked over the figures they had just computed. "Fifteen thousand dollars," Nancy said again.

When Nancy and Susan went downstairs in the early evening, the sorority house had been transformed. The tables in the dining room had been removed to make a dance floor, red-and-white paper hearts were hanging from the ceiling, and a band was setting up its sound system.

Beneath the vases of red roses in the hall someone had placed a sign: HELP YOURSELF. GIVE ONE TO YOUR SWEETHEART!

"I invited Ira to stop by later," Susan told Nancy, looking at the roses.

Nancy smiled at her friend. "Good for you."

Almost everyone in the sorority was downstairs, clustered around the refreshment table, laughing.

"What's the joke?" Susan asked, peering over to the table.

"Harriet made heart-shaped pizzas, with heart-shaped pepperoni," answered a girl as she walked by. "She got carried away!"

Only a few guys were in the room so far, and Nancy saw most of them hanging around out front on the large porch and on the lawn. It must be muscles that get you into Zeta Psi, Nancy observed, recognizing a few of them as members of SDU's swim team.

"*There* you are," Lori called out to Nancy, and waved to her. She told her to come meet the person standing with her in the hall. Lori was dressed in a softer style than usual. She was wearing a pastel flowered print dress with a lace collar. She looked quite beautiful.

"Peter Ryan—Nancy Drew," Lori said proudly. "You two are going to click, I just know it," she said with flushed cheeks. Just then Mike Jamison appeared with one red rose for Lori.

Peter was a handsome guy with shining dark brown eyes, dark curly hair, and a deep tan. Nancy said "hi," and Peter said "click." Nancy smiled at his joke.

"And this is Mike," Lori added. Turning to her boyfriend, Lori explained, "Nancy is checking out the school to see about coming here."

"I enjoyed watching you dive on Wednesday," Nancy said to Mike.

"Thanks," he mumbled, and immediately turned away from Nancy and pushed Lori toward the dining room.

"Ah, young love," Peter quipped. "Today's the day for it."

"Hello, Peter," came a familiar voice behind Nancy. Without turning around, she identified it as Fran Kelly's. "I didn't see you in class last night."

"Which class is that?" Peter asked.

Nancy could tell that Fran was hurt and embarrassed as she answered, "Astronomy. I'm in your lab section." Fran had her hair tied back in a bright red ribbon. She glanced sideways at Nancy as she spoke to Peter. "Last night we used the large telescope at the observatory."

"Oh, no! Was that last night?" Peter asked, putting a hand up to his forehead. "I totally forgot about it. I wonder if I can take a makeup for it."

"Excuse me," Nancy said, and left Fran and Peter.

"I like your hair like that," Kathy said as she met Nancy at the punch bowl.

"Thanks," Nancy said, pouring herself a cup of the bright red punch.

"But your hair looks great no matter what you do to it," Kathy added, tossing her own frizzy curls. "Are you sighing over any of these Zeta Psis?" she asked Nancy.

Nancy shook her head and sipped the punch.

"That one"—Kathy pointed to a tall guy in a fraternity sweatshirt—"is in my calculus class. If I wanted him to be eternally grateful to me, I could share a little secret with him," she said coyly.

Nancy looked down into her punch cup. Although she disapproved of the cheating, she was not comfortable with having set up Kathy and the other girls to fail. She wondered if there was a way to undo her actions before she was caught on Monday.

"Would you feel right telling it out of the sorority house?" Nancy asked Kathy as she considered how to handle the problem.

"I never have before," Kathy confessed. "But I never had such an appealing reason." Turning to Nancy, she said, "Don't worry, nobody will ever know who my connection was." And Kathy headed over to the guy as Nancy watched.

The dance floor was crowded as people paired off. It looked as though everyone had shown up.

After drinking a cup of juice, Nancy went down the back stairway and headed to the study hall. There, on a Friday evening, with the sound of a loud band and a hundred people dancing overhead, sat Alice Clark, a book open in front of her.

"Hello, Nancy," she said as if she had been waiting for Nancy to appear.

"Hello," Nancy answered, walking over to Alice and looking down at the book she was studying. "English grammar?" Nancy asked.

"Linguistics," Alice said in her one-word style.

Rather than ask more questions, Nancy sat down across the table from Alice and waited to see if she was going to volunteer more.

"Interesting," Alice said, still looking at her book, "how many different ways there are of communicating."

Nancy nodded. It was her turn to be quiet and let Alice speak at her own pace.

"For example, one can start a seemingly irrelevant topic," Alice said, fingering the pages of her book, "and still communicate a specific message different from what one is discussing." Still silent, Nancy listened as Alice added, "The purpose of which is to keep the speaker safe."

The pressure points in her physiology text, Nancy thought. It *was* a message to me. It was a piece of information Alice was giving me for a reason.

"And after the message is communicated?" Nancy asked Alice.

Alice said, "Then the speaker and the listener should make no further contact if they want to remain safe."

Nancy stood up and walked out of the basement study hall.

As Nancy reentered the packed dining room, Susan walked up to her. "I was looking all over for you," Susan said. "Please try to let me know if you're going to disappear. I'm jumpy tonight."

"Okay," Nancy agreed. Then she motioned for Susan to follow her into the empty kitchen. Leaning against a cupboard, she whispered, "Alice Clark knows I'm investigating this case."

"She *told* you that?" Susan asked, clearly shocked.

"Not directly. But indirectly, and she gave me some information about how Rina was murdered. I'm convinced she did it on purpose to help me out."

Susan shook her head. "How did she ever discover that you were here to investigate the murder?"

"I have no idea," Nancy said. "And I don't know *when* she figured it out, either."

"Alice Clark is one smart girl," Susan said as the blaring music from the other room stopped. In a much quieter voice, Nancy said, "I'll tell you the details later. But now I think we've got the *how* and *why* of this case. We just need the *who.*"

"Nancy—" Susan began, looking worried. But before she could finish, the door to the kitchen swung open, and Peter stood there with a smile.

"You did sneak in here!" he exclaimed to

Nancy. "Lori told me I could find you in the kitchen." Fiddling with the red rose he held in his hands, Peter said, "The band took a break."

"I heard," Nancy said.

"Want to see the stars with me?" Peter asked. "I'm told there's a deck on the roof here."

"There is a deck," Nancy said. "But I thought you were supposed to look at stars *last* night."

Peter laughed, stepping close to Nancy, and said in a hushed voice, "How could you leave me alone with her?"

"Fran?"

"She had some not so great things to say about you," Peter said. "She's jealous."

Nancy shook her head. "I don't understand Fran Kelly," she said.

Peter put a hand on Nancy's elbow and, looking over at Susan, smiled and said, "Excuse us, please. I want to show your cousin the universe."

As they headed to the rooftop deck, Nancy was relieved to see other people on their way up there. In the twilight she looked out over San Diego. "No stars yet," she said to Peter.

"Fine with me," Peter said, standing close to Nancy and looking at her rather than the sky. Across the deck, another couple were embracing.

For a moment Nancy looked at Peter and thought how good a hug would feel. But it wasn't Peter she wanted to hold her and she knew it.

"You're so lovely," Peter said and gently laid his hand on hers. "Lori was right."

Looking down at the hand that rested on her own, Nancy felt her heart stop. She would recognize it anywhere, even in the darkness. A large ring with a ruby red stone, and the Greek letters, Sigma Kappa.

Chapter

Fifteen

HER PULSE RACING, Nancy pulled her hand out from under Peter's. This guy is dangerous, she thought, glancing at the shaky white wooden railing. Strong and dangerous, and he tried to hurt me once before.

"How about I get us some punch, and we'll meet in my room?" Nancy asked, knowing she'd need help to take on Peter. Help from both Susan and Ira.

"I'd love it." Peter smiled.

"It's on the second floor, right across from the shower room. It says 'Susan Victor' on the door."

"Great," Peter said. "I'll be there, waiting."

I'll bet, Nancy thought. She raced down the stairs to find Susan. After looking around for a moment, Nancy found Susan and Ira on the crowded dance floor. Acting as though she was there to party, Nancy approached her friends and began to dance with them.

"Meet me in five minutes," Nancy mouthed quietly, trying to be understood but not overheard. "Upstairs in your room." Above the sound of the music, Susan asked, "What's up?"

"I've got someone up there, and I might need protection," Nancy explained. "Five minutes," she repeated. "But don't come in right away. Just be there if I need you—please," Nancy said as she headed for the punch bowl.

Lori greeted her there, with a smile. "You and Peter are hitting it off, I see," she said happily.

"He is cute, I have to admit," Nancy said as she poured two cups of the sweet punch. "How did you know we'd like each other?"

"I just *knew* it," Lori said, and Nancy excused herself.

Upstairs, Peter stood with both hands in his pockets looking at the underwater photographs that had been taken by Rina. Swinging around as he heard Nancy approach, he accepted one of the glasses from her.

"How come the most interesting girl in the sorority is only here for a week?" he asked flirtatiously.

"Well, at least we met," Nancy said warmly, and closed the door behind her, being careful not to lock it.

"And how come I'm so lucky," Peter asked, taking the glass from her hand and placing it on the desk next to his, "to be able to have an evening with her?"

Hearing footsteps outside the door, Nancy knew that Susan and Ira were there already. She felt much safer.

Safe enough to say, "That's a lot of questions. Let me ask you one, too, okay?"

"Whatever you like, good-looking."

"How come a Zeta Psi wears a Sigma Kappa ring?" Nancy asked curiously.

"Sentimental reasons," Peter said, fingering the ruby-red stone. "My uncle Joe gave it to me. Anything else you want to know about me?" Peter asked, opening his arms toward Nancy.

"There *is* one more thing," Nancy said sweetly. "Do you always beat up your potential dates before you get to know them?"

"What?" Peter asked, his eyebrows raised, a slight smile on his face as though Nancy had told him a joke. "Beat up *who?*"

"Me, for one," Nancy said, and now there was no sweetness in her voice, just harshness.

"I have no idea what you're talking about," Peter said incredulously, his arms dropping to his sides. "I never saw you before an hour ago."

"I have evidence, Peter, so you may as well forget the lies," Nancy claimed, resting one hand on her hip. "And, I have a deal to offer you. I won't report you to the police if you tell me what that business on the beach was about."

"You're a little crazy, lady," Peter said with a forced smile, "if you think that *I* ever beat *you* up. What 'evidence'?" he asked sarcastically.

"The ring, Peter," Nancy said, looking at him directly. "Uncle Joe's Sigma Kappa ring."

Peter's strong hand swung out and grabbed Nancy's arm. Then she called out "NOW!" and Ira and Susan flung open the door to the room. Peter instantly dropped his grip on Nancy's arm and jumped back.

"My friends," Nancy said, standing up straight. "They also know that it was you who gave me a swollen face."

"I think we ought to call the police, Nancy," Susan said, walking to the wall phone.

"Stop her!" Peter yelled to Ira.

As Susan froze, Peter barked, "What do you want to know, Nancy Drew?"

"I want to know why you did it," Nancy demanded.

"I don't know why," Peter said, glaring at the three of them. "And that's the truth."

"What do you mean," Ira asked angrily, "that you don't know why?"

"I mean," Peter answered, "that I was doing a

119

favor for a friend. I owed him one. But why he wanted me to stage an attack on Nancy and Lori I have no idea." Hesitating, Peter added, "And I didn't ask."

"Who's the friend?" Nancy asked.

Peter silently looked down. Nancy knew that he didn't want to squeal. She casually motioned to Susàn to pick up the phone.

"No!" Peter yelled, putting out a hand to stop Susan. "It's Mike."

"Lori's boyfriend?" Nancy asked.

"Yeah."

"He wanted me and Lori beaten up?" Nancy asked, surprised.

"Nice relationship they must have," Ira said.

Peter turned to Ira and explained, "I was supposed to scare Nancy, not hurt her, and Mike said he'd do the same to Lori. I thought it was a joke between them or something—I don't know. But then Mike let Lori go and slugged Nancy." Looking at Nancy, Peter claimed, "It wasn't my fault."

It looked to Nancy as though she was going to have to hold *Ira* back to prevent him from slugging Peter. "Not your fault?" he mimicked, his hands balled into fists.

"Listen now," Nancy said coldly. "If I find out that Lori or Mike has heard about our conversation, I *will* call the police, and I *will* press charges against you."

As Peter began to walk out of the room, Nancy

had one more question for him. "How are you at darts?" she asked.

"Darts? You mean throwing darts?"

Nancy nodded.

Peter shrugged his shoulders.

"And your buddy, Mike, how is he?"

"I'm finished with your questions," Peter snapped, and slammed the door behind himself.

"Now what?" Susan asked Nancy as the three of them stood looking at one another.

Ira asked, "You think this Peter had something to do with Rina Charles's death?"

"It's possible," Nancy answered.

"And you're a cop, right?" Ira asked.

"A detective," Nancy answered. "But how," she wondered out loud, "did someone figure that out on my first day here? And what does Lori's boyfriend have to do with it all?"

"And what do we do now?" Susan asked.

"We go downstairs and party," Nancy said. "And we keep an eye on Mike and Lori. I think it's their move next. We also have to let our friend Peter know that we're watching him."

"I can't believe that guy," Ira said. "Not his fault—can you imagine? Attacking someone on the beach and claiming it's not your fault!"

Downstairs, people looked as if they were having a good time. There was a lot of loud laughter, singing, and wild dancing.

Nancy saw that many of the girls wore red roses in their hair. The food table had only a few pieces of the heart-shaped pizza left on it, and the band played very loud. All signs of a good party, Nancy thought.

Ira and Susan were also looking around, and the three each headed in a different direction to search for Lori, Mike, and Peter.

But a thorough search of the first floor and outside porch didn't turn up any of them.

"That was quick," Ira said to the girls as they met at the punch bowl.

Nancy nodded. "They're not around anywhere. They've either left the house or they're up in Lori's room."

"So now what?" Susan asked, grabbing a handful of salted nuts.

Just as Nancy was about to answer, she felt something wet drip down her back. "Oh, I'm so sorry, Nancy!" Pam said, and grabbed a napkin to dry Nancy off. The sticky red punch was all over the back of Nancy's hair and dress.

Nancy stopped Pam's attempt to make it better. "It's okay," she said. "Don't worry about it."

Turning back to Susan and Ira, Nancy said, "Why don't you two dance and keep this floor covered. I want to go upstairs and change clothes." Nancy put her hand on the back of her soaking hair. "And dry off. Something tells me that this is going to be a long night."

"Where shall we meet?" Susan asked.

Nancy thought a moment. "Front porch, fifteen minutes," she answered.

As Nancy entered her room, she glanced at the phone hanging on the wall. It would feel so good to talk to Ned, she thought.

No time now, though, Nancy thought, and kicked off her flats, unbuttoned her dress, and dried the back of her hair with a towel. She took a pair of jeans, a jersey, and her running shoes out of the closet.

As she dressed, Nancy sorted through the facts. Mike may have sent Peter to scare me, but, Nancy wondered, who sent Mike? Was it Lori? But why, then, would Lori have gotten attacked, too?

Tying her shoes, Nancy was aware that the music had changed from a fast rock 'n' roll beat to a slow, more romantic one. She looked at her watch. Five minutes before I have to meet Susan and Ira, she thought, and picked up the phone.

As Nancy listened to the ringing of the phone at Ned's house, there was a loud banging at her door.

"So you're the new interim treasurer, are you, Nancy Drew?" came a sing song voice as Nancy replaced the phone on its hook.

"I know you're in there," the voice continued. "Well, all your phony lying can come to an end right now!"

Chapter

Sixteen

Nancy took a breath, flung the door open, and found herself face-to-face with Fran Kelly. Holding a note in her hand, Fran glared at Nancy. "You've got some questions to answer," she said, then added with a smirk, "I've blown your cover, and finally Lori believes me!"

Fran's face was turning progressively redder. "You thought we would never know that you went to the accountant's office, didn't you? I guess you could have never known that Mrs. Haft would tell my mother that some 'nice girl' from Delta Phi came to look at the records. 'Nice girl,' ha!"

Nancy cautiously watched as Fran became lost in her rage.

"And did you really think we wouldn't figure out who you were? Did you honestly think," Fran spit out, "that we would never know that you went to the accountant's office and altered our records? Well, Lori Westerly is not stupid, Nancy Drew." Handing Nancy the note in her hand, Fran said, "But I'm starting to think that *you* are."

In a clear, calm voice, Nancy said, "You've got it all wrong, Fran. And I think you know that."

"I know that Lori finally believes me. I know that she finally trusts me and wants to hear from me." Fran looked at Nancy. "It's funny," she said, her head cocked, her hair and red ribbon hanging over one shoulder. "It seems you may have been my ticket of admission to get in with the right crowd.

Looking at the insecure girl, Nancy realized that Fran Kelly, like Rina, would do anything to get in with Lori Westerly.

It's time to go to the source, Nancy thought, as she opened the note in her hand.

Now is the time to talk.
I'm waiting for you in my room.

L.W.

To Fran she said, "You can tell Lori I'll be right there."

Satisfied, Fran left to carry the message to Lori.

Nancy raced down to the front porch to tell Susan and Ira what was happening, but they weren't there! After a quick look at the dance floor and the kitchen, Nancy felt discouraged —and a bit worried.

Nancy raced back upstairs and wrote a note she hoped they would see. "Lori's room, 11:15," it said.

As Nancy approached Lori's third-floor room, Fran was creeping out. When she saw Nancy, her gray eyes narrowed.

Nancy tapped gently on the closed door.

When she answered it, Lori was no longer wearing the soft dress she had chosen for the party. Like Nancy, she wore jeans, a jersey, and running shoes.

"Come in," she said, sounding friendly. "It seems we have a lot to talk about."

As soon as Nancy entered, Lori's hand closed around her wrist. She turned Nancy, bending her arm painfully behind her back. Automatically Nancy leaned forward, and with one motion untwisted her arm and grabbed Lori's chin to force her to the floor. But Lori didn't fall. She threw Nancy off and remained upright.

In her hand was a sharp metal rock-climbing pick, and she held it with the point lying against Nancy's throat.

"Now, I think we can talk," Lori said, nudging Nancy back against the wall.

"Is this what you did to Rina?" Nancy asked.

"No. With Rina Charles I didn't need anything but my hands. But you're strong. Strong and clever." Nancy could feel the pick still lying at the base of her neck. "But I won't have you ruin my life," Lori hissed.

"She knew you had falsified the financial records and was going to turn you in, wasn't she?" Nancy asked.

"Actually, Rina helped me do it. I told you she was a *good* friend," Lori answered. "But then that pitiful creature decided to run home to Mommy and tattle." She slowly drew the pick across Nancy's neck.

"And she told you before she did it?" Nancy asked to keep Lori talking—to keep the metal point from sliding into her throat.

"Let's just say that I saw signs of her weakening." Lori kept her eyes glued to Nancy. "I understand character.

"You, for example. I didn't believe for one minute that you were visiting the school." Lori smiled. "Not with all your questions about Rina Charles."

"What does Mike Jamison have to do with all this?"

"Oh, now we're getting a little personal, aren't we?" Lori said. "Well, I'll tell you, because soon it won't matter one bit what you know." Lori tossed back her head as she explained. "Mike does what I ask of him. Happily. If I ask him to rough someone up, he doesn't ask why. If I tell him to make sure Susan Victor and her boyfriend are occupied, he says, 'Sure, honey.' How's that for a good guy?"

Nancy didn't answer. It was her turn to worry. To worry about what Mike and Peter were doing at that very moment to Susan and Ira. Nancy worried, too, about how she was going to get out of this situation without their help.

"And if you told him to shoot darts at someone," Nancy asked, her back against the wall, "he'd happily do that, too?"

"I suppose he would," Lori said, her eyes gleaming. "But some things a girl likes to take care of on her own."

"You've got quite an aim."

"I like to do things well," Lori said simply.

Without Nancy's asking any more probing questions, Lori continued. "This is all my baby. Every penny is for my training. It's going to buy me a spot in the training camp. And in the Olympics." Lori's smile faded as she said, "The biggest mistake of my life was telling Rina Charles. But nobody else knows." Glancing at the metal that was at Nancy's throat, Lori added, "And never will."

Nancy stared into Lori's eyes as she quietly said, "You're something, Lori Westerly." Then she raised her knee and slammed it into Lori's stomach.

Taken off guard, Lori buckled but stayed on her feet. Her hand did fall away from Nancy's throat for a second. But instantly she picked it up and forced Nancy into a kneeling position. Dropping her pick, Lori raised her hands and placed her thumbs on two points in Nancy's neck. A tremendous amount of pressure was all Nancy felt before she fainted.

Chapter

Seventeen

WHEN NANCY CAME to, she was lying face-down on a pier, the cold ocean air against her face helping to revive her. She was alert enough to know not to move one muscle as Lori Westerly untied the ropes that had bound her ankles and wrists.

The rest of her body was not cold, and without opening her eyes, Nancy realized that she had been clothed in a wet suit while she was unconscious. The movement she felt on her back was undoubtedly an air tank—empty—that Lori was adjusting. Nancy could feel a bulky weight belt around her waist. That would certainly take her deep into the Pacific Ocean.

Time, Nancy thought. I need a little more time to get my strength back. Just take your time with the finishing touches, Lori.

But Lori seemed in a rush. In less than a minute, she was finished. Nancy could sense her standing up and heard her brush her hands against each other, as though she had just completed a job well done.

Nancy's hands felt numb and cold from the lack of circulation when they had been tied at the wrist. She's untied me now, though, Nancy thought, so when my body is found, there won't be ropes around my hands and feet.

But my body isn't going to be "found," Nancy thought with determination and rage. It's going to walk out of this situation and be alive enough to turn Lori Westerly in!

With that, Nancy powerfully swung out one leg and sliced into Lori. At the same time she grabbed one of Lori's feet and yanked with all her might.

Caught completely off guard, Lori fell back. Despite the weight of the air tank and heavy belt, Nancy jumped to her feet. Plunging into Lori with all her strength, Nancy pushed her down flat onto the pier.

"You are dead," Lori hissed, and pushed Nancy back with remarkable power after grabbing her wrists.

"No, I'm not!" Nancy insisted, one knee on the pier and one knee pushing into Lori's solar plexus as she held her down. "This is what you did to Rina, exactly what you did to Rina. But not again, Lori Westerly!"

Suddenly the night was filled with light, and both Nancy and Lori had an instant of shock. Then Nancy heard a voice, Susan's voice, screaming out, "Nancy! Nancy! Are you here?"

"On the pier!" was all Nancy could shout. Lori struggled with incredible strength as Susan and two police officers got out of a Jeep and ran toward them.

"It's all over, Lori," Nancy said, moving her knee. "One murder is enough."

As the officers surrounded them, Lori began explaining, "She's flipped out. She asked me to help her with her diving equipment, and then she attacked me."

One officer looked at the air tank that was strapped to Nancy's back. "Can we see that?" he asked.

Nancy slipped off the air tank, and as he examined it she took off the heavy weight belt as well.

"Empty," was all he said as he snapped handcuffs on Lori. "We need to take you down to the station now." They led Lori, her face turned away from the others, to the waiting Jeep.

"Are you all right?" Susan asked, her voice cracking. "Oh, I'm so glad we found you!" she said, hugging her friend.

"I'm fine," Nancy said, "How did you ever figure out where to find me?" she asked Susan.

"Before I went out to the porch to meet you, I went in to use the bathroom," Susan explained. "Ira was to go out to meet you. But when I got outside, he wasn't there; neither were you."

Susan took a breath as she continued her explanation, and Nancy saw that there was another policeman standing at the foot of the pier. He looked as if he was waiting for them. "I saw your note," Susan continued. "Then I went to Lori's room and saw it was in a shambles. I knew something terrible had happened. So I decided to think like Nancy Drew"—Susan looked at her friend—"and it worked."

Nancy smiled. But Susan didn't return her smile. She looked worried. "They still have Ira," she said.

"Who has Ira?" Nancy asked, alarmed. But then she answered her own question. "Mike and Peter!"

Susan nodded. "It must be them. They must have taken him as he walked out the front door."

"Yes. Lori said they were supposed to keep you occupied," Nancy said out loud, remembering. Then she declared, "Well, now it's time to search for *him!"*

The two girls walked together to the end of the pier.

"I'd like to take you home now, girls," the policeman said.

"Thank you," Nancy agreed, looking down at the heavy rubber wet suit she was still wearing. "I'd better get in some clothes." She and Susan went with the officer to the police car that was on the pavement above the beach.

As the police radio gave out reports in the car, Susan nervously asked their driver, "Did you hear anything about my other friend yet?"

"Nothing yet, but don't you worry, miss," he said, trying to reassure her. "We've got a slew of men out looking for him."

"We want to join the search," Nancy declared. "As soon as I can get out of this thing."

"I'm afraid I can't let you do that," the policeman said protectively. "I'm heading back to the station to go off duty. I was supposed to go home three hours ago. Did you know it's two in the morning?" As he pulled into the sorority house parking lot, he said, "You two just get some sleep now. We'll let you know as soon as your boyfriend shows up."

Nancy and Susan headed up the stairs of the dark, silent house. "Get some sleep," Susan whispered angrily. "Is he kidding?"

In their room Nancy and Susan spoke in hushed tones as they tried to piece together what they knew.

"That's how Lori murdered Rina, isn't it?" Susan asked sadly. "Exactly the way she was trying to murder you."

"Yes," Nancy said, her hand moving up to her

neck. "She pressed on my throat until I passed out, just as she had done to Rina."

As Nancy unzipped the tight diving suit, she said, "But I had a whole lot more warning. I knew I was dealing with a potential killer. Rina thought she was with her best friend."

"And Mike," Susan asked, her voice shaking. "Is he a killer, too?"

"No. Absolutely not. He has no idea about any of this. Lori told me it was 'all her baby.'" Looking at Susan, Nancy said, "I'm sure Ira is safe. Mike and Peter just do what they're told."

"Same as Rina," Susan added, shaking her head. "Lori Westerly is one powerful person."

"How did she ever get me into this thing?" Nancy mumbled, trying to pull the tight sleeves off her arms. "Especially unconscious."

"They all just followed orders," Susan said, helping Nancy. Thoughtfully, she added, "It sure makes you think about following your own beliefs and not someone else's orders."

Changing into her gray running pants and jacket, Nancy nodded her agreement.

As Nancy began to tie her shoes, Susan said, "You have no intention of staying here and waiting, do you?"

Nancy smiled. "What's that you just said about following your own beliefs?"

Susan laughed with relief.

"The only question now is, where do we go?" Nancy asked, dressed and ready. "Mike and

Peter could have taken Ira anywhere. They could have just gotten in the car and driven him up the coast. Lori's instructions were only to keep him occupied."

"I just had an idea," Susan said with some hesitation. "It may be a little off the wall, but—"

"Go ahead," Nancy said eagerly. "Sometimes in this business, those leads that just come to you out of the blue are the very best ones."

"Well," Susan said, "I was thinking that the captain of the swim team might have a key to the gymnasium. What do you think?"

"I agree!" Nancy said, and headed to the door, ready to go.

There was silence on the campus at that hour, and deep silence around the huge gymnasium. Susan and Nancy circled the building and tried every entrance, hoping to find one unlocked.

"That car," Nancy whispered to Susan, pointing at a light blue sedan that had been parked in a tow-away zone near the back of the gym. "That car was in the sorority parking lot during the party, I'm sure of it."

"Then they *are* here!" Susan exclaimed, keeping her voice down.

"Maybe," Nancy whispered. "At least *somebody* is here that was at Delta Phi earlier today."

The girls headed over to the car to see if there was anything in it that might identify who owned it. A sound startled them as they had just about reached it, and instantly Nancy grabbed Susan's wrist, dragging her into the dark shadows behind the car.

"She didn't say we had to baby-sit for him *all night,*" a voice said out loud, totally unaware of being overheard. Peter's voice. Nancy recognized it.

"There's no place he can go now, anyway," Mike agreed. "Not in the condition we left him. I'll free him before practice tomorrow."

Putting his key in the passenger side of the car to let Mike in, Peter said, "I don't like that guy. You should have seen him tonight in Drew's room, pretending he was a big hero."

Silently the girls watched in terror as Nancy feared that Peter would walk around the rear of the car to go to the driver's seat.

But Peter stayed where he was as he asked Mike, "Do you think Lori will care that we didn't get the girl?"

From inside the car, Nancy could hear Mike respond, "Nah, I think it was *your* girlfriend she was after. Lori has had business with that Nancy Drew since she got here. Something about her being sent from the national office to cut back on Delta Phi's finances."

What a story, Nancy thought. Susan shook her head in disbelief.

"Lori just needed some time to straighten her out," Mike added. "I'm sure she's had enough by now. It's the middle of the night."

As Peter headed toward the front of his car, Nancy felt her own rapid heartbeat.

In moments the car had pulled away, leaving Nancy and Susan alone on the dark pavement. As Susan began to head toward the gymnasium, Nancy said, "Stay down, they have a rearview mirror."

When the car had safely pulled away, the girls stood up and headed for the gymnasium. They were frightened for Ira's safety. What had Peter and Mike done to him?

As Nancy was examining a low, barred window, a flashlight hit the building directly in front of them, and a voice called out, "What's going on over there?" Swinging around, Susan and Nancy saw a campus security guard approaching.

"Our friend is in there," Susan explained, almost talking too fast to be understood. "And we're afraid he's been beaten up. Please help!"

"This building's been locked since nine o'clock," the guard said, a pile of keys jangling on his hip.

Briefly and as calmly as they could, Nancy and Susan told him what had happened and of the two boys who had just pulled away.

"Yeah. I heard the car," the guard admitted. "That's why I came by to check." Taking the keys off his belt, he said, "Okay. Let's see what we've got in here."

Entering the pool area, the three of them searched the bleachers. Susan, her heart pounding, made herself look at the bottom of the pool, and was relieved to see nothing.

"The locker room," Nancy suggested. The girls headed back there as the guard continued to search the pool area.

"Listen," Susan said, her movements freezing.

"To what?" Nancy asked after a moment of silence.

"I thought," Susan said, "that—"

Nancy and Susan heard the moans at the same time, but Susan was the first to scream, "Ira!"

"He's in a locker!" Nancy shouted, and then ran for the guard. "We need the keys, quick!" she called to him.

Susan stood outside the small locker. "We're here, Ira. We're here. We'll get you out!"

The guard moved as fast as he could to find the right master key for the lock.

Finally he forced the locker open and there was Ira, stuffed into the cramped small locker, gagged and bound, his face bleeding.

Chapter
Eighteen

In the infirmary, Ira got his face cleaned and bandaged, his bruised ribs taped, and some pain-killing medicine pumped into him before the girls took him back to his apartment.

Although Nancy and Susan got only a couple hours of sleep, by eight the next morning they were awake and talking in their beds.

"When Ira hugged me," Susan said, "I think that may have been the happiest moment of my life. To know that he was alive, and not badly hurt." Shyly Susan added, "He's wonderful, isn't he?"

Nancy fluffed up the pillow behind her head

and smiled at her friend. "He does seem pretty wonderful," she agreed.

"I've been thinking about your cover," Susan said to Nancy. "I wish it were true. I wish you were considering coming to SDU."

Her bright reddish blond hair shining against the pillow, Nancy smiled. "I'm afraid I love my work too much," she answered. "But it has been wonderful to be with you again. I'm glad you brought me in on this case."

"You were incredible, Nancy." Susan rolled onto one elbow and looked at her friend. "I truly will never forget this experience. I appreciate your work so much! If I hadn't found out the truth about Rina's death, I couldn't have lived with myself."

At the gentle knock on the door, Susan called out, "Come in." Debbie and Patty, dressed, and carrying a thermos and mugs, came in.

"Perfect," Nancy said, sitting up and smelling the hot coffee. "Just what I need to get me out of bed and packing."

"We heard you talking," Debbie explained apologetically.

"And there are rumors flying around this place a mile a minute already," Patty added. "You have to duck if you don't want to get hit with one." Setting the coffee on the desk, she said, "So we thought we'd better come to the source of the controversy."

Just as Susan and Nancy began to fill them in on the events of the night before, the phone rang. Susan jumped out of bed to answer it, and Nancy could see by her smiling face that it was Ira. "That'd be great," Susan said. "If you feel up to it." Covering the phone, she said, "Ira and Larry want to come with us to the airport. Okay with you?"

Nancy nodded. "Great. I'd love to say goodbye to them," she said, and returned to her conversation with Debbie and Patty.

"We thought," Debbie said, "that you had come here in connection with Rina's death."

"But after you asked us about the exam stealing, we thought that maybe Rina's death was related to that."

"So did we," Nancy said, folding some clothes and laying them in her suitcase. "But it was a blind alley."

Nancy turned to Debbie. "You knew something about that, didn't you?"

Once more Debbie reddened. "A few months ago, I was invited to join the inner circle. 'We need someone like you for some of the special things we're doing,' Lori said to me."

"Like murder, I guess she meant," Patty said dryly.

Nancy saw Debbie give a little shudder at the word before she continued. "Lori and Kathy asked me if I could get my sister to give us the marine biology final. She's a TA in that department." Looking down at her hands, Debbie said, "But I'd never put Shelly in that position, and I told them that."

"So *that's* why they've been so rude to you?" Patty asked her roommate. "You never told me this before."

"I never told anyone," Debbie said quietly. "But now is the time for telling."

"So those people who have tomorrow's calculus exam . . . ?" Patty asked, sipping her coffee.

"Those people have my friend's idea of what he hopes will never show up on the calculus exam," Nancy answered.

The four girls couldn't help but burst into laughter.

Pouring Nancy another cup of hot coffee, Patty asked, "What happens to Lori now?"

"That's up to the courts to decide," Nancy said. "I'm wondering about her henchmen —Mike and Peter."

"Well, the word downstairs is that they were caught and booked for assault and battery and kidnapping. They were picked up at the Zeta Psi house," Debbie explained.

"The rumor is that they denied everything." Patty continued. "Said they don't know anything about anything."

"Well, I think it's time to stop the rumors, and tell the facts around here," Nancy said. "As Debbie said, it seems that now is the time for telling."

After Patty and Debbie left the room, Nancy asked Susan, "Which is Alice Clark's room? I'd like to talk to her before I leave."

"She's got a single upstairs on the third floor, if she's not in the basement study hall."

Alice looked pleased when she opened her door and saw it was Nancy standing there. "Come in," Alice said.

"Have you heard the rumors?" Nancy asked, walking into Alice's small room.

"Yes." The other girl nodded and sat on the edge of her bed. "It sounds like the case is solved now. Want to sit down?" she asked Nancy, gesturing to a cushioned chair across from the bed.

"Thanks." Nancy smiled. "Yes. The case is solved, but there are still some things I can't explain."

Alice waited, looking down at her feet.

"How did you know about the pressure points?" Nancy asked directly.

"It's public record," Alice answered. "I didn't believe that Rina's death was an accident, and I guess your cousin didn't, either. Is she really your cousin?" Alice asked, looking up.

"No."

Alice nodded as though confirming her guess. "Anyway, I went to the police department and asked to see the coroner's report. It said the cause of death was drowning, but it also mentioned two darkened spots on the front of the neck." Alice looked down again after she had finished talking.

"So you were trying to solve the case, too?" Nancy asked, encouraging the shy girl to talk more.

"Yes. But when I saw that Susan had brought in a real private eye, I decided to hand the material over to you." Alice looked back at her as she said, "Nice work, Nancy."

"Thank you. But how did you know I was a detective?" Nancy asked.

Alice shrugged. "Nobody else talks to me much. You asked a lot of questions and were friendly, and I could see you wanted as much information as you could get. I figured," Alice said, "that you were either a detective or a very nice person." Looking at Nancy, she said, "You seem to be both."

"Thanks," Nancy said warmly. Then, smiling, she added, "I do ask a lot of questions, don't I? I have one more, if you don't mind."

"Fine." Alice shrugged.

"Was becoming treasurer the way you thought you could best investigate?" Nancy asked.

Alice nodded. After a moment's hesitation, she told Nancy more. "I decided to speak to Lori about my abilities. Especially my ability to keep a secret, and I was sure she knew that I don't talk a lot." Alice looked around her small room. "When Lori pushed for me to be elected, I knew I was headed in the right direction."

"Nice work on your part, too, Alice."

"Thanks," she said. And for the first time that Nancy could recall, Alice Clark smiled.

"Listen to this, from page eight of Monday's campus newspaper," Larry said, holding up some papers.

"Monday's newspaper?" Ira questioned.

Larry nodded. "The editor's my good friend. I spent a couple hours with her this morning. This is the layout for Monday's paper."

The four young people were sitting at the San Diego airport waiting for the announcement of Nancy's plane. It seemed to Nancy that longer than a week had passed since Susan met her here.

And now, in a matter of hours, she would be back home. Nancy had finally reached Ned, and he was going to pick her up at the airport when she arrived. "With open arms," he had said on the phone. "And maybe even a belated valentine."

"'Our source, a reliable graduate student,'" Larry began, reading from the paper in his hand, "'has reported a method of exam pilfering that has apparently become common in some circles.'" As Nancy, Susan, and Ira listened, Larry went on to read in great detail about the cheating scheme that involved "small cliques of manipulative students" and "cooperative teaching assistants."

"And now he wants us to guess who the

'reliable graduate student' is," Ira said, holding Susan's hand in his.

"Good for you!" Susan said excitedly, ignoring Ira's teasing of his best friend. "You took it to the authorities!"

"I couldn't resist," Larry said, and continued reading. "'The chancellor's office said it will recommend suspension of any student or faculty member involved in such behavior.'"

"I think it's great that you reported it," Nancy told Larry.

"Thanks," Larry said, pleased. And then he added, "I do wish I could have caught someone red-handed, though."

"But you had the courage to make it public," Nancy said. "And that will certainly scare people away from participating. That's very important."

"Coming from you, a fellow detective," Larry said slyly, "I'm delighted with the compliment."

As Susan and Ira laughed at his mock pompousness, Larry added, "Which reminds me. There is another article in here you might be interested in seeing." Larry then showed them what would become page one. The headline read: UNDERCOVER DETECTIVE EXPOSES MURDER. Glancing at Nancy, Larry read, "'Nancy Drew, called in to investigate what had looked like a scuba-diving accident, has given evidence to the police linking the "accident" with a fifteen-thousand-dollar embezzlement scheme.'"

"Front page again, Nan," Susan said with a smile.

"I'm very impressed with your work, Nancy," Larry said sincerely.

"Thanks," Nancy said. "From a fellow detective, I really appreciate that."

Ira laughed out loud, and then put one hand to his side, where he was wrapped up from the fight the night before.

"It only hurts when I laugh," he said lightly to Nancy. "Don't look so worried. You've been in worse shape at least twice this week!"

"I'll send you a copy of the paper when it comes out," Larry said. "If you'd like."

"I would," Nancy said, knowing her father would love to see the article. Nothing gave Carson Drew more pleasure than hearing about his daughter's adventures.

"Flight Seven-fourteen now boarding from Gate Twenty-nine," came the announcement over the loudspeaker. Nancy stood and stuffed the SDU shirts that she had bought for Bess, George, and Ned into her carrying case.

"That's your flight, isn't it?" Susan said sadly.

"I'm afraid it's that time," Nancy answered as they all stood up.

Susan reached into her own bag and brought out one of the beautiful underwater photographs of Rina's that Nancy had so admired. "I thought this might help me say thank you," she said quietly. "I can't tell you how much I appreciate what you did. You're a wonderful friend, Nancy."

With a lump in her throat, Nancy took the gift and hugged her old friend. "And I can't tell you how glad I am that I could be here," she said softly.

As the other passengers filed into the waiting plane, Ira and Larry also hugged Nancy goodbye.

When she was the only one left to board, Nancy grabbed her bag and headed up the hall, turning back to smile and wave one more time.

It wasn't until she was in the air that the wave of sadness passed. Looking out the window at the vast ocean far beneath her, Nancy's feelings shifted to the very special, deep satisfaction she always felt after having solved another mystery. Nothing can quite compare to it, Nancy thought, watching the Pacific disappear as the plane headed inland.

Leaning her head back against the cushioned seat, Nancy Drew looked out over floating clouds. Soon the plane will land, Nancy thought with a smile, and Ned will be there with open arms.

Nancy's next case:

"If you are blond, blue-eyed, and feminine-looking —and like to wear white—I must meet you immediately. I promise you won't be sorry."

This is the personals ad that Bess Marvin answers. But she *is* sorry—her blind date threatens her!

Can Nancy crack this newspaper case—or will she end up in the obituaries? Find out in *VERY DEADLY YOURS*, Case #20 in The Nancy Drew Files℠.

Enid Blyton
Five Find-Outers
Mystery Stories
in Armada

ARMADA

Other titles by
Enid Blyton
in Armada

ARMADA

All these books are available at your local bookshop or newsagent, or can be ordered from the publisher. To order direct from the publishers just tick the title you want and fill in the form below:

Name _____

Address _____

_____

Send to: Collins Childrens Cash Sales
        PO Box 11
        Falmouth
        Cornwall
        TR10 9EN

Please enclose a cheque or postal order or debit my Visa/ Access –

   Credit card no:

   Expiry date:

   Signature:

– to the value of the cover price plus:

UK: 80p for the first book and 20p per copy for each additional book ordered to a maximum charge of £2.00.

BFPO: 80p for the first book and 20p per copy for each additional book.

Overseas and Eire: £1.50 for the first book, £1.00 for the second book. Thereafter 30p per book.

ARMADA